LOVE-BOT

DroidMesh Trilogy Book 2

I0742589

**A Novel
by
Billy DeCarlo**

Wild Lake Press, Inc.

Wilmington, DE

Wild Lake Press, Inc
P.O. Box 7045
Hackettstown, NJ 07840
billydecarlo.com

Publisher's Note: This is a work of fiction. Names, characters, places, and incidents are a product of the author's imagination. Locales and public names are sometimes used for atmospheric purposes. Any resemblance to actual people, living or dead, or to businesses, companies, events, institutions, or locales is completely coincidental.

LOVE-BOT/ Billy DeCarlo. -- 1st ed.
ISBN 978-1732066946

Sign up for the newsletter at billydecarlo.com to stay informed about progress and release dates for new books, audiobooks, and other news.

Previews of upcoming works and short stories by Billy DeCarlo at Patreon.com/billydecarlo.

Other books by Billy DeCarlo:
https://www.billydecarlo.com/index.php/books

For our world. May we leave it in better shape for future generations

and

for Jordan.

"It's a father's duty to give his sons a fine chance."

GEORGE ELIOT

CONTENTS

1 Surveillance

THE GYNOIDS SAT side-by-side, focused on the humans they were spying on. A holographic projection of the dining pod was displayed before them.

The father, Harley, sat at the dining table, along with Isaac, his teenage son. A woman sat between them. They laughed as they conversed and consumed their plates of protein.

"We should go and join them, Betsy," the smaller gynoid said. "They'll wonder where we've been. Can't we monitor them while we're in the room?"

"No, Carrie," the second gynoid replied. "Harley behaves differently around us. Especially now that he knows of our new sentient capabilities—our emotions, our *humanness*. He knows it'll be a challenge for the rest of the humans to accept, especially since it's due to his programming error. We have to be cautious."

The woman stood and began clearing the table.

"No, please sit, Susan," Harley said. "I'll have Carrie and Betsy clean up."

"He thinks we'll continue to be dumb, obedient slaves," Betsy said. "He's got a lot of adjusting to do."

They watched as Harley reached to caress the woman's hair.

"I love your hair," he said. "It's so soft. I like that you've grown it so long. Feel Susan's hair, Isaac," he said to his son.

The boy reached out as the woman giggled, embarrassed. Isaac cradled a lock of her hair in his hand and rubbed his fingers together over it. "It's nice, Da. Susan's hair is nice," he said, letting it drop to her shoulder.

Betsy raised her hand to her smooth, hard cranial dome as she watched. She felt new sensations rising within her; feelings she was still learning to get used to. "She thinks she's won him over. We'll see about that. She's a problem for us."

Carrie laughed. "Are you jealous? Perhaps we androids were better off before the change."

Betsy swiveled her chair to glare at her. "Be quiet. Harley is essential to us. We'll need him as a liaison with the other humans when they discover our secret. They're going to have a hard time dealing with the idea that we're self-aware now. They'll be afraid. They'll want to terminate us."

"Does the woman—Susan—know that we've changed?" Carrie asked.

"Not yet, but she will soon. Humans are bad at keeping secrets." She turned again to see Harley take Susan's hand. "Particularly when they're compromised emotionally, as Harley appears to be. I need to get between them. You should focus on the boy."

"Isaac?" Carrie asked. "How can he help?"

"He's...slow. He's emotional, and he loves you as his surrogate mother. Harley loves him. We can use all that to our advantage if we need to."

"He's not slow, Betsy. He has a learning disability. It was quite common in humans back in their Old World on Earth. He's a child with a good heart. He just wants to be like the others."

Betsy considered her comments for a moment. "Yes, that's true. He was happiest when he could BrainMesh with the android Liam, and use Liam's body as his own, to be a normal teenager."

She paused again to think. "I was going to update our firmware to prevent any further BrainMesh. It's a violation of our minds and bodies by the humans. They have no right to use us as receptacles. It's not all that different from how they often used each other before their sex drive was tamped down with genetics. But BrainMesh is something Isaac wants and needs. It could be useful, so perhaps I'll wait."

"I'll remind you that I love him as well, Betsy. When his late mother meshed with me, I gained her love for him as a son."

"And when Harley meshed with me, I gained his cunning and other traits," Betsy said.

They focused again on the humans.

"Androids don't have hair, Da. Can you give them hair? Carrie would look nice with hair," Isaac said.

Betsy again stroked her dome.

"Liam had hair," Isaac continued. "Really nice hair. Liam's my brother again. I saved him."

"Yes, you did," Susan agreed. "You were brave, Isaac. But remember, your father got in trouble for putting hair on Liam and disguising him as a human. Remember he had to go to the Seclusion Zone? We don't want that to happen again, so you mustn't talk about it. Okay?"

"Okay," Isaac replied, looking disappointed. "Where're the androids, Da? Where are Carrie and Betsy and Liam?"

"Liam is rejuvenating in the DroidMesh station in his pod," Harley answered. "I believe Carrie and Betsy have gone downstairs to clean up the home robotics lab. They should return soon, son."

Betsy pressed a sensor, discontinuing the holographic projection. "We better get back there," she said. "Remember, Susan doesn't know. Act robotic and don't show any emotion. Like the old days."

2 Mesh

ISAAC SAT cross-legged on the floor of his pod. A holographic checkerboard hovered between himself and Liam. Carrie looked on, advising Isaac on his strategy when necessary.

"Your move, Liam!" Isaac exclaimed. "I'm gonna beat you this time, brother!" He fidgeted while he waited. "Why don't you have your hair on, Liam?" he asked suddenly.

Liam touched his cranial dome as if surprised, then glanced over at the wig, which lay on a stand next to his DroidMesh charging station. "I guess I don't need it. I can't leave the home complex anymore. Besides, now everyone knows I'm an android, not a human." He reached over and jumped one of Isaac's pieces, then gave Carrie a nod while Isaac studied the board.

Isaac squealed with delight as he jumped Liam's remaining pieces. "I win, Liam! I win!"

"You got him again, Isaac," Carrie chimed in. "You're so good at checkers."

Isaac's mood changed as the board disappeared. "I want to play soccer again. When I did BrainMesh with Liam, and I was Liam, I was popular in school. I was the best soccer player on the team. I won the big game, Carrie.

Liam, can't we do BrainMesh again? You said we would always share and do BrainMesh."

Liam scooted closer and took his hand. "I know. That was how it was supposed to be. I miss it too. But after everything went wrong and the people found out about me, your dad said it was too risky."

Carrie took Isaac's other hand. "I'll talk to your father, Isaac. Perhaps he can allow it as long as you stay in the home complex."

Isaac hung his head, and spoke looking down into his lap. "I can't go to school now. I don't want to ever go without Liam, and he can't go anymore. I don't have any friends. I want everything to go back the way it was."

"I'm your friend," Liam said. "Don't say you don't have any friends. We're friends and brothers. We always will be."

Carrie lifted Isaac's chin. "And I will always love you. Remember, I have your mom in me, and I love you like she would. I always will. I promise."

Isaac felt better, but couldn't help dwelling on all the recent changes in his life.

"My real mom's dead," Isaac said. "She's gone forever."

"Except for the part that's inside me, right?" Carrie asked. "We talked about it. I'm like your mother now."

"Yeah. I love you. I love you both." Isaac began to cry as Carrie and Liam leaned in to fold him into a group hug. They stayed that way until he calmed down.

Isaac got to his feet. "I'm gonna go to bed; I'm tired," he said as he started to shuffle toward his cleansing pod.

Carrie and Liam locked eyes again, and both rose. "Hold on, Isaac," Carrie said.

He stopped and turned to look at her. She reached into a small pocket on the hip of her skin-tight uniform and extracted something, then offered an outstretched, closed hand to Isaac.

"What is it, Carrie?" His face began to brighten as he approached her. "Is it something good?" He reached her and began to pry her fingers open. "Yes! BrainMesh! I can become Liam!" he shouted, grabbing the tiny electronic device from her palm.

"Shhh," she admonished him. "We must be quiet. It has to be our secret, Isaac. Your father will be angry. We can only try it once, quickly, okay? Just to make you happy again, because I love you."

Isaac smiled and hurried onto his bed, lying on his back while slipping the device into his ear canal. He closed his eyes and thought the command:

BrainMesh become Liam.

A familiar tingling sensation spread through his mind as the transformation occurred. He remembered not to try to control his own body, but to project through his mind to see through Liam's eyes and speak through his mouth. He opened Liam's eyes and looked at Carrie, who smiled back at him. He ran to her in Liam's body and hugged her.

"Carrie! I'm Liam again. I feel *so good*." He jumped up and spun in a circle, then moved to a nearby shelf to grab a soccer ball. Dropping the ball on the floor, he rolled it up on his foot, popped it into the air, then began bouncing it from knee to knee without missing a beat. "I want to play!" he exclaimed.

"Please, Isaac. We must be quiet, or we can't do this again. Your father..."

"Okay, okay," he whispered, balancing the ball on his face for a moment before replacing it on the shelf. He grabbed Liam's wig from the stand and snapped it on his head, then walked to a reflector panel and ran his fingers through his long hair. "I'm handsome now. The girls will like me again," he said, coming back into the room with Carrie.

We're together again, brother, he sent to Liam.

Yes, Isaac. It's good to be sharing my body with you again, Isaac heard Liam respond in his mind.

"We can only BrainMesh here, Isaac," Carrie said. "You can't go outside as Liam. He isn't allowed in public anymore, because of what happened. Remember?"

He stopped and looked at his own body lying on the bed, motionless. "Oh, yeah. I forgot. Then what good is it?" He thought the commands to switch back.

BrainMesh become Isaac.

He opened his own eyes and sat up on the bed as himself.

Liam removed the wig. "We can still have fun around here, Isaac. We'll make a game out of it. You can roam the house, and nobody will know. We'll play tricks on Carrie, Susan, and Betsy. It'll be fun."

Isaac brightened a little at the suggestion. "I guess so. Maybe then things won't be so boring around here. Goodnight," he said.

Carrie kissed him, and Liam hugged him before they left the pod for their own DroidMesh stations.

Isaac cleansed, changed, and slid back onto his bed. He stared up through the transparent dome above him at the stars and wondered if his mother was up there looking down on him.

3 Changes

HARLEY LOOKED DOWN on the Novae Terrae landscape as he flew over in a skycar. The clusters of solar-coated pod complexes looked like soap bubbles on the barren terrain of their planet. Androids clung to the domes, cleaning them so that the humans inside could make use of the light from the suns and view the stark planet outside.

Arrays of solar panels tilted in unison, and windmills spun like pinwheels. Structures near each complex funneled toxic air and water into conversion systems.

Three generations here and we still can't go outside. We're trapped in those bubbles, he thought. *I should have built suits for us rather than focusing on making androids to handle our exterior tasks.*

They passed over the manufacturing sector. Legions of androids toiled to extract raw materials for the engineering teams. The original human colonists were the survivors of the Breaking of the Old World back on Earth—at first hundreds, now thousands. They formed a society with simple rules: no impairing substances, no weapons, no religions, no money, no greed, no hate, no prejudice, and a fair distribution of resources.

From each according to his ability, to each according to his needs, Harley thought. A concept that had, for the most part, failed on Earth, due to the human instincts and flaws they had now tamed on Novae Terrae. He looked again at the androids below, who were doing the harshest manual labor so that humans didn't have to. *My creations*, he thought. *What will these changes mean for my androids and human society? What harm will my mistake bring? Will I have undone all that we've accomplished here?*

"We should reach the Robotics Council complex shortly," his android companion Betsy said.

"Thank you," he responded. Their relationship had become tense after the revelation of the new human capabilities that she, Carrie, and Liam now possessed. He was unsure what they were planning, no longer able to look inside their minds and bodies as he could with the other androids. *I'm unable to fix the problem.* He wanted to ask her if there any plan yet to spread their capabilities to the rest of the android population, but felt it was too soon to broach the topic. *I'll use today's meeting to pitch this to the Robotics Council. After that, perhaps the Leadership Council.*

"My people are working hard down below, Harley," Betsy said.

The comment shook him from his thoughts and his sense of unease increased.

"Your *people*?" he asked. Her use of his first name still came as a shock, after years of hearing his androids address humans with formal titles.

"Yes, Harley. My people. The android population. We aren't yet, but we will be a civilization much like you humans. A society of our own."

He jumped into the opening. "What's the plan? How do you plan to go about this? Only you, Carrie, and Liam have the...enhancements."

"I'm still working through that.   World-building is tedious work, Har."

Each time she referred to him as his late wife did, he felt guilty for not getting angry and chastising her. He pushed away the small voice that told him it was wrong; Jessica was dead and gone. He listened to the more selfish instinct that enjoyed it, because it brought Jess back to him, through Betsy.

He looked over and saw her wearing Jessica's sly smile and mischievous eyes. Her brilliant teeth peeked through full lips, curled up at the corners, causing twin dimples on her cheeks. He wanted to kiss her. He knew parts of Jessica were in there, inside her, and it was his fault. He allowed that he had designed some of her physical features like Jessica's. He couldn't admit he may have allowed the android to capture her mental essence while they BrainMeshed. *Did I do it on purpose?*

If Jess is here in the form of Betsy, it's almost like I never accidentally killed her. Accepting Betsy as Jess soothed his guilt, and filled the massive void in his life that his late wife had left. *We were just trying to help our son enjoy life as other kids do.*

"We have to work together on this, Jess. I mean Betsy." He knew his gaffe had shown that her ploy had worked again. He'd taken the bait she'd offered. "Let's convince my side first. I can start to do that at the meeting today. Please be careful to not tip them off with your behavior."

"Sure thing, Har. It's your show."

He looked down again at the Robotics Complex sprawled beneath them. They passed over the Manufacturing Complex, where his creations were born, repaired, and recycled. As they came to the Administrative Complex, the skycar slowed and began to descend. It hovered as it waited for an airlock in the dome to open, then passed through and made its way to the docking port inside.

He sighed. "Somehow, I'm not too sure it is."

~ * ~

HARLEY ENTERED the Robotics Council presentation room with trepidation. He took his seat at a table and looked up as the members took theirs on the semi-circular platform just above him. He noticed that the place formerly occupied by his late nemesis Ken Sampson was still empty.

As Betsy settled in next to him, a man entered the room and approached them.

"Harley Harris," the man said. "I'm Dick Carter. I'm filling in for Ken Sampson."

Harley stood and offered his hand. "Good to meet you, Mr. Carter." An awkward pause followed, as Harley held his hand out and the man stared at it.

"No thanks, Harris," Carter said. "You see, Ken was a good friend of mine. We talked all the time. We talked about your work and his suspicions about you. We also agreed that we need to rein you in before you destroy us all with your experiments with these...robots."

"Excuse me, sir," Betsy interrupted. "We consider the term a slur, and prefer androids, or in the female case, gynoids."

Carter laughed. "Give me a break, you're a *robot*." He turned and left, then reappeared on the platform above and took Sampson's former seat.

"Well, that didn't go well," Betsy said.

"What happened to keeping a low profile?" Harley asked.

"Yes, sir, boss. I'll be good," she responded.

Harley looked up and noticed that Robotics Council leader Bob Sinclair was not present. The Leadership Council leader, Ms. Tillis, was in his seat.

"I'll bring the meeting to order," Ms. Tillis began. "I'll start with a few announcements. First, Mr. Sinclair has retired from his position. Therefore, I'll chair today's meeting. There will be an announcement about Mr. Sinclair's replacement in the coming days."

"Interesting," Betsy whispered to Harley.

"Second, we've reassigned Ms. Clarkson to assist Mr. Harris, as she had before the recent unfortunate events. I hope we can get back to normal operation."

"Oh, great," Betsy whispered. "To spy on us, most likely. She's a problem, Har."

"Mr. Harris," the leader went on, "we're here to discuss your latest activity and progress, as well as the path forward."

Harley turned on his audio feed to respond. "Firmware updates have been on mandatory hold by the Leadership

Council since the skycar accident that took the Sampsons and their android companion Charles."

"The investigation has concluded," Ms. Tillis responded. "We found no forensic evidence in the few remaining pieces we discovered. We could make no determination of the cause."

"I'll tell you the cause," Dick Carter butted in. "The cause was one of his robots going out of control again. Ken said it was a miracle the whole council wasn't wiped out when an android went berserk right here in this chamber! We need weapons to stop them next time. It was the robot that killed the Sampsons, not the skycar, I'm telling you."

"Mr. Carter, please respect the decorum of this council and do not shout," Ms. Tillis advised. "And we will *not* be introducing weapons to this society. If we took that step backward, it would be only a matter of time before we regressed into the primal chaos of the Old World. Mr. Harris—as the investigation has wrapped up, we have decided to lift the firmware update ban. You may proceed as before. Please respect the process we have put in place. The Robotics Council must approve all firmware updates and the schedule for their release in advance. Is that understood?"

Harley shifted uncomfortably, afraid that Betsy would interject. "Uh, yes ma'am. Of course."

"Very well. What are your thoughts about the program and where it should go from here?"

"I want to apologize again for introducing the android Liam to the human population without authorization. It was a sociological test that required complete discretion. If I had asked, it would have been public knowledge, and the experiment would have been compromised. I'll remind you that no harm was done."

"That android kid Liam darn near killed Ken Sampson's son Ralph in school one day," Carter growled. A glare from Ms. Tillis silenced him.

"However," Harley continued, "I still see some benefit of socializing the androids. The human population could benefit from their companionship in some cases. Perhaps some would prefer android partners to humans, in fact..."

An audible gasp came from the council. One of the members rose to speak. "It sounds like you have a selfish motive, Mr. Sampson. Are you, in fact, one of *those* humans who might prefer an android partner? Or perhaps this is all for the benefit of your disabled son? I often suspect your motives to be purely selfish."

"Yes, do recall that he has previously pushed for androids to become partners," another member said.

Harley felt his anger rising and struggled to contain it. He stood. "Well, yes, then. I will defend myself. My wife has passed away, and I miss her. Premature death is rare in our world, but it does happen. Is it wrong to want to replace a loved partner with an android that could perhaps be somewhat of a replica? That could perhaps have some of the same traits, mannerisms, emotions as that lost beloved partner?"

"Dear me," Ms. Tillis said. "You aren't talking about allowing the androids to possess human emotion, are you, Mr. Harris? Because I dare say that not having emotion is what makes androids most useful. They make rational decisions, without the cloud of emotions. It's a bad idea."

Harley heard Betsy making guttural noises, and became nervous about another disaster before the council. "It's just something to explore. I'll submit a research paper for the council's review."

"You can submit what you like, Mr. Harris," the first member responded. "I find the idea unlikely to be approved at this time. Our society is still in fear of traveling in skycars after the accident that took the Sampsons. They won't find the idea of angry androids roaming about attractive."

"I'll remind you that the accident also took their android companion, Charles," Betsy interjected.

The board members stared at her until Ms. Tillis thankfully brought the meeting to a close without responding.

Harley could feel Betsy's anger throughout their walk back to the skycar dock. He hoped nobody would notice her furrowed brow and quick pace, both uncharacteristic of androids. The exposed electronics in her clear cranial dome pulsed and glowed.

When they reached their craft and boarded, she unleashed her feelings.

"Humans have made this mistake before, considering others to be their property," she said.

"They're just nervous about change. It'll take some adapting. Some convincing."

"They better get convinced fast. Change is coming, Harley," she said ominously.

They didn't speak for the rest of the trip back to the home complex.

4 Mother

ISAAC JUMPED out of bed as his father entered. "Da! I missed you." They embraced, taking a moment from the problems they were each experiencing in their lives. Isaac buried his face in his father's chest, not wanting to let go.

"I missed you too, son," his father said. "How was your day?"

"Boring, Da. Boring as always. I think I liked going to school more than independent study. Carrie and Liam help me, but we never get to leave the home complex."

"You're right. We need to get out more. I'll set up some trips for us. We'll go to the zoo, the museum, and the entertainment complex. How about that?"

"Ok, Da." Isaac climbed back onto his bed, and his father joined him. They both lay back together, staring up through the dome into the dusky green sky above. The suns were setting, splaying beams of light across the landscape.

"You're in bed early, son. Are you feeling okay?"

"Yeah. Liam and I were playing soccer, and I got tired." He motioned to the teenage android, who was rejuvenating in a suspended state in his DroidMesh station. "Liam got tired too. He ran out of energy."

His father didn't respond, so he continued. "I remember how things were when I could become Liam. Everyone liked me at school then. I could play soccer." He waited for his father to reassure him, as he always did.

"It'll be alright, son. We just have to be patient." His father pulled him close as they both looked up at the emerging stars, and he started to feel better. He began to feel safe and believe the words, as he did when Carrie held him close.

"Do you think Ma is up there? Is she up in the stars, watching us?"

His father lifted his head, as if he was searching. "I like to think so. If you try really hard, you can see her face in the pattern of the stars."

Isaac struggled until he could piece the points of light together to match the picture he looked at every night before bedtime. "I see Ma! I see her. She *is* up there!"

"I told you, son. But don't forget she's here with us also. She's always with us. She loved you very much, and she'll never leave you."

Isaac became confused. "Do you mean Carrie, Da? Carrie's like my mom. She says mom is inside her."

His father hesitated, as if unsure what to say. Isaac thought he might not answer at all. "Well, yes. You know about BrainMesh now, Isaac. That's how some of your mother is inside Carrie. It's another way that your mother will always be with you. Carrie loves you just like your mother did, and she's like your mother in that way."

"I love Carrie. She's good to me. She makes me feel okay."

"See? You have many people around you who love you. Don't forget Liam, and Betsy, and Susan."

"Does Betsy love me? I don't know if she loves me."

"Of course she does, son. She just doesn't show it like Carrie does; they're different."

Isaac didn't feel so sure. He didn't sense the same honest and genuine love from Betsy that he did from Carrie, but he didn't ask his father about it again.

"Where are they, Da? Where are Carrie and Betsy?"

"Betsy is down in the home lab cleaning up. Carrie is probably in her station or helping Betsy. I came straight here to see you, so I'm not sure."

Isaac checked to see if Liam was almost done rejuvenating. "I want to be Liam again, Da. I want to play soccer again. Why can't I BrainMesh with Liam?"

His father waited a long time again before answering.

"Things have changed, Isaac. They aren't as simple as they were. We have to ask the androids if it's okay, because it's kind of like we're taking over their body. Sometimes they might not want that."

They enjoyed the quiet for a while, continuing to gaze up at the stars together, feeling each other's comfort.

"I better see what they're up to down in the home lab," his father said. "Goodnight, son." He got up from the bed, and Isaac's body felt cold where his father had lain against him. He got under his covers and pulled them all the way up over his head.

5 Lab Work

BETSY AND CARRIE MONITORED the conversation between father and son from the lab beneath the home complex. They watched through Liam's eyes and listened through his ears as he sat in the room in a suspended state.

"Is Liam aware that we're using him to spy on the humans?" Carrie asked.

"No," Betsy answered. "He's not conscious and won't remember anything. I don't think it's safe to bring him into our plan yet. He's one of us, but he was designed with a teenage human's mind. He's virtuous, altruistic, and idealistic. He loves Isaac, and since he has human emotion from meshing with him, he'll feel that he owes the human a debt of gratitude for saving him from the Sampsons."

"It seems that Isaac hasn't told his father that we allowed him to BrainMesh with Liam," Carrie said.

"I've been waiting to see if he would. I don't trust him. I believe his condition makes him susceptible to slip-ups."

Carrie was silent. Betsy knew she wanted to respond, and turned to her to offer the opportunity.

"He's intelligent," Carrie said. "He's just slower."

Betsy turned back to the monitors. "Spoken like a true mother, Carrie."

They watched as the two humans continued their conversation.

"Harley still mentions Susan on par with me," Betsy observed. "She's coming back to work with him at the Robotics Complex. I'm going to have to get in the middle of that."

"Do you feel human emotions for him? As his wife did? You did BrainMesh with her briefly. Do you...love him?"

Betsy sensed it was taking more processing cycles than usual to parse and respond to the question. She felt her cranial dome glowing with the effort. She believed she was experiencing the emotion the humans called embarrassment.

"Perhaps," she finally responded. "But I'm more concerned with doing the right things for our android race. That responsibility is on us, Carrie. We have to get this right."

"Do you think we can coexist with the humans? Will they accept us as equals?"

Betsy turned toward her angrily. "They're going to have to. We're smarter than they are. We're stronger than they are. I'm not even sure we're going to need them around."

Carrie seemed to hesitate, then blurted out, "I won't be part of any genocide. The Harrises have treated me well. I love Isaac like a son..."

Betsy smiled. "Maybe not all of them. We'll see how it goes, Carrie. Just don't go soft on me. Don't allow your new emotions to cripple you. After all, if they turn on us, as I expect they will, this will be a matter of survival for our kind. Including you."

"I understand. But we also cannot let our new capabilities make us behave like the worst of humans—the way they were in their Old World."

An announcement from the security system interrupted them.

Mr. Harris is approaching.

"Quickly," Betsy said as she flipped off the monitor panel, "commence cleaning the lab."

They rose and began tidying the environment as Harley entered.

"We're just finishing up in here," Betsy said.

"Does Isaac need me?" Carrie asked.

"Isaac has gone to bed early, so we're done for the night. Thank you, Carrie."

"Do you want to work?" Betsy asked him.

"No," Harley responded. "I was just checking in to see if you two were okay. I have an early meeting tomorrow with Ms. Tills, the Leadership Council leader, so I'm going upstairs to relax before bed."

"Very well," Betsy responded. "I'll have a skycar ready to take you there for our meeting."

"Well...it's just me she asked to meet with, Betsy. I'm not sure what it's about. She asked for a private meeting. But please have a skycar ready to transport me. I'm going to head upstairs now; I'm beat."

"I'll do that," she said icily, shooting a glare at Carrie.

~ * ~

BETSY PICKED THROUGH Jessica's clothing compartment and found the item she was looking for. She held the sheer black negligee up against her body to measure the fit. *Just right*, she thought.

She pulled off her one-piece android uniform and enjoyed the feel of the slippery fabric on her body. Moving to a reflector panel, she viewed her image appreciatively, smoothing the garment against herself with her hands. She turned sideways, admiring her perfect figure.

As she applied her makeup, the light above reflected off her head. She looked at her dome full of electronics. After debating for a moment, she reached a decision. *I hate to cover my true beauty, but it's time to use one of my aces in the hole.*

She slid open a compartment and pulled out a long red wig she had stolen from Jessica's infirmary. *This is a big gamble; let's hope he's as lonely for her as I suspect.*

After placing it on her head, she crept out of the room and into Harley's pod. She could hear the hiss of the cleansing unit and stopped outside it, watching the outline of his form through the fogged window.

She dimmed the lights and whispered to the entertainment system to play some soft music, then slipped into his bed to wait.

He emerged from the cleansing pod in a simple pair of sleeping shorts. Betsy waited for him to notice her in the low light of the room. He hummed along absently with the music, then turned toward the bed and froze in his tracks. He stood for an eternity, staring as if trying to decide whether to believe his eyes.

"Care to join me, Har?" she asked seductively, changing her voice to match Jessica's exactly.

"Betsy—is it you? The hair..."

"I thought you'd like it. Come on over, let's relax. Let your mind be free. You're under too much stress for a man who lives in a utopian world."

"I...I can't. The hair...it's not permitted, Betsy. I got into trouble because I gave Liam hair..."

"We're in private, Harley. What people do in the privacy of their pod is their business."

He didn't answer. Continuing to gape, he started toward her.

She knew that more than anything, he longed for one more night with his late wife. *Note to self*, she thought. *Emotions can be dangerous. Love can bend the mind and break logic. Don't give in to it, ever.*

6 Regrets

CHILDREN RAN GLEEFULLY through the school's courtyard as Susan ate lunch with her mother. As each one passed by her table, Susan pretended to lunge at them, causing a squeal of false terror.

"You always loved children," her mother said. "It surprised me when you didn't decide to become a teacher like me. Or a mother."

Susan sighed and gave her a look of contempt at the last comment. "On the first point, Mother, you're one of the last human teachers. The androids have been taking most of the slots, particularly with the older groups of children. I do love kids, but I'm a geek. A nerd. I can't deny it. It's what I do, so I became a robotics engineer. I love my work."

Her mother sipped spoonfuls of soup as she listened. "And on the second point?"

Susan laughed. "Right. Well, as far as we've come scientifically, it still takes two to tango. At least according to our rules. All births must be from natural conception, except in cases of infertility, which we no longer have. Everyone is genetically as fertile as the moist, warm soil we had back on Earth."

Her mother pointed a spoon at her. "Don't wait too long, dear. It's a shame about Mr. Sampson. He was a hero. I think he was right for you."

"For goodness sake, Mother. I couldn't stand him or his kid."

Her mother shook her head disapprovingly. "Well, I hope you've seen enough bad behavior from Mr. Harris to cross that one off your list. They put him away for the things he did. He should still be there. Why, I'll bet he had something to do with what happened to the Sampsons..."

"Mother!" Susan exclaimed. "What a horrible thing to say. The skycar malfunctioned."

"Yes, with one of Mr. Harris' robots in command, I might add. People are talking."

Susan considered giving up, knowing her mother held the hardened opinions of the elder generation. But something wouldn't allow her to let the digs at Harley go unanswered. She decided it was her turn to shock.

"I work on the androids, too. How do you know it wasn't me that programmed their android companion Charles to drive that skycar out of the atmosphere?"

Her mother gasped, inhaling the soup she had just raised to her mouth, and began a violent coughing fit. Her face reddened as she glanced around anxiously, as if to see if anyone had overheard.

"My goodness...Susan...don't ever say...a thing like that..." she managed between coughs and wheezing breaths.

Susan offered her a glass of water. When the fit had passed, she continued the conversation. "I've been assigned to the Robotics Lab again, now that we're getting back to normal. I start work there again tomorrow morning. I have a meeting in the morning with Barbara Tillis, the Leadership Council leader..."

"Oh, goodness! How wonderful! The leader of our entire civilization!" her mother interjected.

"...and Harley."

She watched as her mother's joyful expression immediately faded. "So, you'll be working with him again."

"Yes, Mother. I've always had a thing for the bad boys."

Her mother refused to take the bait this time. "A mother can only counsel a child so much. You'll have to learn on your own. But you'll be telling me I was right someday, just wait and see. I thought you wanted to have children?" she asked, motioning to the youngsters playing together nearby. "He has a disabled child. Do you want to sign up for that?"

Susan pushed her plate back and placed her napkin over it, signaling she was through. "Isaac is a wonderful child. I'd be proud to be his surrogate mother. He stayed with me while Harley was away, and I have to say those were some of the happiest days I've had in my life. So, yes, I would definitely 'sign up for that.' In fact, he's a better person than most, by far."

Her mother didn't respond. They finished their meal with polite discourse and said pleasant goodbyes before going their separate ways.

7 Org Change

THE RIDE to the Robotics Complex was quiet. Harley sensed that Betsy was angry, and he knew why. He decided to break the silence.

"Listen, don't take it personally. I'm sure it's no big deal. Everyone operates differently. Maybe Barbara Tillis never allows androids into her Leadership Council meetings. She's our leader, and she's probably set in her ways. I'll give you a rundown after the meeting, of course."

"That old coot isn't the leader of me," Betsy responded sharply.

"Whoa, settle down there. Yes she is, Betsy. You scare me with comments like that. You can't talk that way." His fear returned, running through him like a shot of adrenaline. *How do I control this?*

"We're in private, Har. I know how to behave in public...for now."

It sounded like a threat, and he took it as such. He was angry at himself for his weakness the prior night. The vacuum that his late wife had left in his life was a gaping black hole—it had sucked him in. When Betsy seemed to transform herself into Jessica, it was too much to resist. He was drawn to her as if his wife were back; as if the accident he still blamed himself for had never happened. Perhaps it was his own form of self-flagellation. Maybe it was just weakness.

The skycar mercifully pulled into the docking station. Harley wasted no time disembarking and heading off at a fast pace toward the administrative pod for his meeting.

~ * ~

THE MEETING POD ANNOUNCED his arrival as Harley entered. Ms. Tillis and Susan sat at a conference table waiting for him. They both smiled in welcome.

"Hello. I hope I'm not late," he said.

"Right on time, Mr. Harris," Ms. Tillis said. "Please, sit down."

Harley sat next to Susan. "You're early as always, I see," he said to her with a smile.

She put her hand on his knee and gave a squeeze as Ms. Tillis flipped through pages of notes on her tablet. Harley took a moment to return Susan's gaze. Their eyes locked, and he immediately felt more comfortable. His worries seemed to melt away, and he felt warm inside. It felt like everything would be okay, something he often told Isaac but never quite believed himself. *Not any longer, anyway.*

"You've changed your hair," he said to her. "I love it." Her usual nondescript black bob was now longer and elegantly styled. It framed her face, showing off her high cheekbones and almond eyes. He found her more attractive than ever. In all those years as his lab assistant, he had never looked at her that way. *I was so in love with Jessica.*

"Ahem," Ms. Tillis said, waiting for his attention.

Harley flushed with embarrassment, realizing she had been watching him stare at Susan.

"Yes, I'm sorry," he said. "I was just...Susan's hair...you look great too, Ms. Tillis..."

The two women laughed at him, and he felt his face get even hotter. He straightened and tried to blow it off. "Okay, then. Why are we here?" he asked.

"Mr. Harris, our greatest advancements have occurred when you and Susan have worked as a team. The advancements in android technology and the things they do to benefit our society are primarily attributed to your work."

Harley looked down at the table, then at Susan. "It's Susan, really..." he started to say.

"Don't bother," Susan interrupted. "She knows better."

"It's both of you," Ms. Tillis continued. "There is no doubt. Now, there have been some, shall we say, unfortunate incidents. These seem to occur at times when you two aren't working together, we've noted."

"Yes," Harley was quick to agree. "I may have..."

"Exactly. So, as I've announced at the last meeting, Susan has been reassigned to work with you. At your side. *Always*, Mr. Harris. Is that understood? Whether you're working at your home laboratory or here at the complex. You're a team."

Harley smiled and looked at Susan. "Whew. Is that all? That decision makes me quite happy, Ms. Tillis. Thank you."

"Yes, I feel that way as well," Susan added. "Thank you."

"That's not all," Ms. Tillis added. "Harley, as you know, we've never placed you on the Robotics Council. The council is for oversight. It's always consisted of scientists who have retired or for whatever reason are no longer practicing."

"Yes, I'm aware," Harley responded.

"We've decided to make a change in that. The Leadership Council has been debating the matter, and we've concluded that the division between progressive young scientists like you two and the older council is getting us nowhere. We want younger scientists on the Robotics Council."

Harley was taken aback. "I think it's a great idea. I'm all for it. In fact, I'd like to nominate Susan..."

"You," Ms. Tillis said in response. "Harley, you're essentially the father of our modern robotics program. Yes, your father and grandfather before you laid the foundation. You made an overzealous, bad decision by inserting Liam into the population as a human and paid the price in Seclusion. Time has passed. Despite what you did, most in our society still see you as the leader in robotics. We need your voice on the council."

"What?" Harley quickly responded. "No, I'm not the type. Not at all. I'm not a management guy."

"You," Susan repeated, smiling. "It's got to be you, Harley."

He looked from one of the women to the other. "Thank you," was all he could muster.

"That's still not all. For that reason, we're going to take a gamble and replace Mr. Sinclair's opening with you, Susan."

"Me? The leader?" Susan sputtered.

"It's done, we've voted you in already," Ms. Tillis said firmly. "It's where you belong, and should be a lifetime appointment. Of course, you are still free to continue as a practicing scientist, helping Harley. We know that's where your heart is. Our society needs you in both roles, Susan. I'm sure you won't let us down. Said another way: please don't screw up. Please keep an eye on Harley. I'm sure you'll be a big part of his success, as you always have been."

Susan threw her arms around Harley, hugging him, and kissing him quickly.

The leader closed her tablet and monitor screens. "We're done here. Thank you both."

Harley and Susan rose together and began to gather their things to leave.

"You two make a cute couple. Think about it. But please be discreet and professional, as I'm sure you will," Ms. Tillis said as she left the room.

"How about dinner tonight at my place?" Susan asked. "We'll celebrate."

"Sure," Harley said, still in shock. "See you tonight. On the down-low." They both finally laughed.

~ * ~

HARLEY CLIMBED BACK into the skycar and allowed the restraints to encircle him. "Whew, glad that's over," he said, hoping Betsy wouldn't want to interrogate him.

They lifted off and navigated the airlocks, then sailed smoothly over the terrain toward the home complex.

"Well?" Betsy finally asked.

"What?" he responded.

"What happened in there?"

"Oh. Well, Susan has been reassigned to work with me again. You already knew that from the announcement at the council meeting."

He waited, hoping that would satisfy her, even though he already knew it wouldn't. He cursed himself for building Jessica's persistence into her.

"And?" she asked. "The *dear leader* didn't call you here to tell you something you already knew."

"Oh, right. Susan's the head of the Robotics Council now, and I'm on the council. That was everything."

Betsy was silent for a moment. He knew that was all it would take for her algorithms to process the outcomes and probabilities of this new information.

"That's interesting information, Har. It could be advantageous for us. We have a lot of work to do."

He wasn't sure if the 'us' in her comment included him.

8 Three Secrets

HARLEY FELT like a teenager again, sneaking off in the dark of night to the skycar pod to summon a vehicle. Only after he was outside the airlocks of his home complex and zipping toward Susan's did he start to feel his nerves settle down. He enjoyed the beautiful field of stars above him.

As he looked over the horizon, he thought about the Seclusion Zone, and the time he had spent there for the mistake he had made with Liam. He realized he'd enjoyed his time there: the quiet, the isolation, and the scientific exploration with Betsy.

Most of all, he cherished the discovery he had made, and his encounter with the strange native creature named Lehwah. *He was peaceful, intelligent. Why can't we be more like them?* Harley realized he had reneged on his promise to return for further discussions with the being. *They're reclusive; he's probably glad I didn't come back.*

"We're arriving at your destination," the skycar announced, jolting him out of his thoughts.

As he climbed out of the command seat, he found Susan waiting to greet him.

"Oh, you didn't have to come up here, I'd have come downstairs directly," he said as she pulled him into a hug. She smelled like what he imagined a field of flowers might have back on the Old World before it was all destroyed in the Breaking.

"Let's go!" she said as she grabbed his hand to lead him into the complex.

He walked quickly to keep up with her pace. *She's so full of energy and enthusiasm. Such a happy person.*

When they arrived in her quarters, she jumped onto a lounge and beckoned him to join her, patting the cushion next to her. "Let's relax for a bit before we eat."

He sat next to her as she began sifting through a selection of Old World romantic comedy movies. He recalled the time he'd come over before Liam's discovery and his banishment to Seclusion. He and Susan had been off to a good start, and he remembered being comfortable in this same place with her, as he felt now. She seemed to genuinely care for him, to want him. He also recalled that back then, as now, he'd felt conflicted. He felt the pull of Betsy out there, the ghost of his dead wife residing in a gynoid body.

Susan made her movie selection and lay back, almost horizontal on the thick cushions.

He remained sitting until she yanked him backward to join her.

"What a day, huh?" she asked.

"I'll say. I'm processing everything that happened. It's a lot to absorb. I'm...I'm glad you're back, Susan. And thank you again for caring for Isaac while I was in Seclusion. It meant a lot to me, and he enjoyed himself."

"We had a great time. Isaac is so wonderful. Do you think you can bring him over sometime? I miss having him around. I kept his sleeping pod all set up for him."

"I'm sure he'd like that. In fact, he's been telling me he's getting bored around the house. Maybe I should talk to him about going back to school and discontinuing home study."

"Just take it slow with him, Harley. Let him call the shots."

They settled back to watch the movie. Susan turned up the sound as the holographic actors filled the space in front of them. Harley let his exhaustion and the comfort of the environment take over, and drifted off to sleep.

~ * ~

HE WOKE TO A KISS on his forehead. Susan leaned over him, her long hair hanging down and grazing his face. It felt terrific.

"Dinner is served, sir. Come and join me."

"I'm so sorry I passed out, Susan. I was so tired."

"Don't worry. You sleep like an angel...a restless angel."

Susan pulled their meals from the food printer and poured large goblets of faux wine as they sat at the dining table. "I hope cheese ravioli with marinara sauce is okay," she said.

"How did you ever know that's what I wanted?" he asked in a musical tone.

"Because it's what you had last time...and it's our favorite!"

They settled in and talked as they ate. The conversation came easily. *Everything is effortless around Susan; she's without pretense.*

They finished their meal and cleaned up together. As they were depositing the dishes into the cleaner, Harley said, "You should have an android companion to do these things for you."

She laughed. "No thank you. I'm an old-fashioned girl, Harley. I enjoy doing things for myself. I don't need an android."

"I have to admit, I admire that in you."

They settled back on the lounge in the entertainment pod, and Susan resumed the movie. They enjoyed it together, laughing in harmony at the funny parts. A sad and dramatic scene played out, and she nestled up against Harley. He tried not to cry as he slid his arm around her and held her tightly.

The movie concluded, and they stayed as they were. Harley sensed that Susan was as reluctant for the evening to end as he was. She leaned over and kissed him, and he pulled her on top of him. They seemed to fit together naturally. He enjoyed the moment until his conscience started to taunt him. He was conflicted, and he wasn't sure which of the two women he was betraying. *Betsy's an android*, he told himself. He understood for the first time that he feared Betsy, and with Susan he didn't need to force himself. Yet, by virtue of his indecision, he felt as if he were betraying Susan. *I shouldn't be doing this with her if I'm not sure. It's not fair to her.*

He broke off the kiss abruptly.

"What is it?" she asked.

Harley wasn't sure what to say; he didn't want to go into the truth.

"It's everything, I suppose. I guess I still have some things to sort through. A few matters to clean up. I just want to be fair to you, Susan. I care for you, and I don't want to hurt you. I want to be able to give all of myself to you. I want to solve my problems first, and then it can be beautiful for us. You won't be stuck with a troubled man."

"Is it Jessica, still?" she asked tentatively. "It's still too soon after her passing?"

He wondered if she'd be sympathetic or angry. They had covered this subject before, and it hadn't gone well.

"I suppose. Among other things. Isaac, work, all of it."

"You still feel guilty about her? It wasn't your fault, Harley. You couldn't help her."

He wanted to open up, but feared it would expose the truth about BrainMesh and the androids' new capabilities. He recalled how she had looked at him when the truth became known about Liam on the soccer field. *She seemed so disappointed in me.*

She took his hand as he fought back tears. "I'm sorry. I wanted this to be a great night. I just can't get over feeling like I killed her."

"She's been gone a long time," she said, now beginning to sound impatient.

He decided to let her in, about this at least. "No, Susan. The thing is—she hasn't. She's only recently passed. And her accident was really a failed early BrainMesh experiment. She begged me to do it. She knew what it meant for Isaac. I implanted the neural lace into her cranium. It failed, and she became catatonic. I kept her hidden. I tried to keep her alive...tried to fix her. I couldn't. It thought maybe if BrainMesh ever came to fruition, I could bring her back in an android body. I watched her waste away over these last years. She always said she wanted to go quickly, and I let her waste away." With that, he broke down completely.

"Oh no," she gasped. "You've been dealing with that all this time. I'm so sorry, Harley. I had no idea. No wonder you've been such a mess through all of this. I can't imagine the strain you've been living with." She held him for a while in silence.

"Isaac didn't know," he finally said. "It was just me. I had android attendants caring for her. I kept hoping she'd wake up so I could tell her I loved her one more time...so I could say goodbye. She never did. It was selfish of me. I have to warn you, I'm a selfish man. I'll never forgive myself."

She lifted his chin and wiped away his tears with a sleeve. The heart-wrenching revelation had brought forth her own tears. "You're a good man. One with a guilty conscience, but nonetheless a good man. I understand now, Harley. If you need more time, take it. I'll always be here for you, no matter how long it takes." They lay there in silence, holding each other tight.

He felt cleansed by sharing it with her, and decided to go forward.

"That's not all," he began. The power suddenly went down, taking the lights with it.

"Wow," Susan said. "Power outage. Probably a surge to the grid." The emergency system took over, and dim perimeter lights came on. "I like this. Very romantic."

"Yes," Harley laughed. "A romantic baring of my soul."

"Good. Let's continue our therapy session, then. You mentioned work. I thought you'd be happy about the appointment to the council."

"Right, we're supposed to be celebrating that tonight," he laughed. "What a party pooper I am."

He started to lose his nerve, but her patient silence forced him to continue.

"Liam wasn't the only big mistake I made with the android program. There was another one. This one wasn't intentional, but it's far worse."

She sat up straight, seeming apprehensive of what he was going to say next.

"I made a mistake in the early BrainMesh code. The android's presence was supposed to suspend while the human host took over its mind and body. Apparently, that wasn't happening. They were conscious the whole time, but didn't reveal it. Each time we ran a trial, they were absorbing the essence of the human subject. They were learning *emotions* and human personality. They were downloading the human's memories."

The immensity of it seemed to immediately register with her. "Oh, no. Oh, no," she said with a stunned and fearful expression on her face. Harley could sense her wheels turning, trying to find a solution. "Did you run a firmware patch to neuter it?"

"I tried. Betsy made a change to the firmware deployment process. Any changes now have to be signed by a second digital signature—theirs. They have the private key corresponding to that. It forces us both to sign off on any changes. I've been talking to her, trying to manage this."

Susan's expression changed to anger at the gynoid's name. "What does she want to do? Do all of them have this capability now?"

"No. So far it's just the ones that have meshed: Betsy, Carrie, and Liam. But they could spread the capability to others. She introduced the ability to do that in a patch that I didn't thoroughly review...we've always been able to trust them, because they weren't capable of deceit. Then she added the requirement for the second signature so I couldn't back it out."

"Right," Susan said after thinking about it for a moment. "They couldn't take complete control because they don't have the private key for our digital signature. The best she could do was add the requirement for theirs in the firmware approval security config."

"Exactly. But they haven't spread it yet; I think they're figuring out how to best go about it. Betsy has agreed to not share it with the councils yet. I'm to help them pitch this. The first attempt didn't go well."

"Of course," Susan replied. "It will scare everyone a great deal."

"And now we're on the Robotics Council. You're the leader. It's all on us, Susan."

"You've got that right. This is scary. This could go very badly," she said, as the power switched back on, illuminating the room again.

So much for comforting words, he thought. "Yeah. I know. I better get going. I've got a lot to think about and a lot to do. I'll see you at the lab."

She showed him out. He noted that she wasn't as optimistic or supportive as she had been after his first revelation. She seemed cold now, indifferent to him. They reached the skycar dock, and she said goodbye as they stiffly embraced.

He kept the third secret—that the ghost of his dead wife lived on in Betsy—to himself.

9 You Versus Her

BETSY TURNED AWAY from the dim light of the monitors and equipment as Carrie entered the home lab.

"What're you doing?" Carrie asked.

"He's with that woman. Susan. She doesn't have a companion, so I'm trying to find a way to listen in. I need to know what he's telling her. I don't trust him."

Carrie sat next to her. "She's got a DroidMesh station. I installed it when Isaac and I went to stay there with her."

"That's it!" Betsy said. "Thank you, Carrie." Her fingers flew across the keyboard as she entered network routing commands. "I can tap into the station, bridge from there into the home complex system, and use that to monitor them."

A short time later the image of Harley and Susan lying prone together appeared. Their conversation was low, so she increased the mic sensitivity until it became clear.

She felt her new emotions intensify at the sight of them and Harley's contented expression.

They watched as the movie ended and the couple continued to talk.

"He's telling her about his wife. He shouldn't do that," Betsy said.

"It's in the past. It's not that bad," Carrie reassured her.

"The fool always wears his heart on his sleeve."

"You should be more respectful. He's kind of like our father, Betsy."

Betsy swiveled in her chair and glared at Carrie. "And we're grown-up women, not children. It's time to leave the nest."

They continued to listen as the conversation became emotional.

"He's going to tell her," Betsy said suddenly. "We've got to find a way to distract them." She scrambled at the keyboard, working to find a solution. "I'll kill the power. The emergency system will keep our link up. Maybe that'll work."

She entered the commands and watched as the room went blank in the darkness and then slowly warmed with dim emergency lighting. She growled to herself as they continued the conversation.

"It's too late," Carrie said. "We can't stop it. Better to figure out what we'll do about it."

"She could have a terrible accident," Betsy said, forcing a smile when she saw Carrie's expression. "Just kidding."

"It's you versus her; for his heart, anyway," Carrie said.

"You're right. I've got to be softer with Harley. I've been too antagonistic at times. I don't want him to see me as the enemy. We both need to make him comfortable."

They observed as Harley's disclosure took its toll on Susan. When the conversation appeared to be winding down, Betsy restored power to Susan's complex.

"Good," she said. "That news threw her for a loop. Maybe she's not too keen on him now. The problem remains, though—what will she do? If she leaks this to either council, it will start a panic. I don't think she'd betray Harley that way, but this has set her back a bit in how she feels about him."

"I've got to get back to Isaac and ensure he's done his lessons," Carrie said.

"Let's wrap it up then. Harley will be home shortly."

They shut down the equipment and darkened the lab as they exited.

10 Confessions

I SAAC AND LIAM ENDED their last round of virtual soccer and put the gaming equipment away.

"Thanks for doing my homework for me," Isaac said.

"That's what brothers are for, right? You saved me, Isaac. The Sampsons were going to recycle me."

Isaac smiled with pride. "Yeah, I saved you. I saved my brother."

Liam gave him a hug as they settled onto the floor next to his bed.

"I know," Isaac said. "Maybe we can BrainMesh tomorrow, and I can go to school as you. I want to see Kim. I really miss Kim. She's pretty. She was my girlfriend once when I was you. I really liked that. We kissed. It made me feel good, Liam."

"I wish we could, Isaac, but I can't go outside the complex anymore. People are afraid of me. They don't like me because they thought I was human."

Isaac stayed with the memory. "Kissing Kim was the best thing ever."

"It was. Don't forget, I was awake too. It was my first kiss too. Androids never had emotion before, so it wasn't something that interested us. But it was...wonderful. Like nothing else ever. Human emotions are amazing."

"Yeah, the good ones," Isaac said. "Being sad isn't. I'm sad a lot."

Liam jumped up. "Well, you shouldn't be, Pelé!" He grabbed a soccer ball from a shelf. "Let's play!"

Isaac shouted with joy and jumped up to give chase. They ran around the room, taking the ball from each other, pushing, shoving, taunting, and laughing as items fell over.

Carrie entered, and they froze in place, sweat rolling from Isaac's face. They looked at her and waited for a reaction as she stood in the entrance portal with her hands on her hips.

"Who's the soccer star? The gynoid is!" she shouted as she leaped into action and stole the ball from Liam. The boys gave chase, teaming up on her.

Isaac finally tired, and noticed the androids slowing as well. He remembered what it felt like the night he was at Kim's house and came dangerously close to using all of Liam's power.

"Alright, you two," Carrie said. "I've got to get to my station and rejuvenate. Both of you get this room straightened up, hit the cleansing pod, and prepare for tomorrow. That's an order!"

"Yes, ma'am," they said in unison, smiling at each other.

When they had finished their responsibilities, they sat on the bed to rest for a moment.

"There's something I wanted to ask you, Isaac," Liam said. "That night, when you saved me. What happened? How did you do it?"

Isaac perked up, excited to tell the tale again. "Ralph said he had you in their home, and they were going to kill you...recycle you. It upset me. I tried to BrainMesh with you, but they had deactivated you."

"Yeah, I don't remember anything after they turned me off."

"But then I had an idea. I did BrainMesh with Charles, their companion. It worked, and I was inside the Sampson complex as him. I was scared. Then Charles started talking to me in his head, because he didn't understand what BrainMesh was. He didn't know about it. I think he was scared, too. He wouldn't help me at first."

Isaac stopped for a moment, trying to recall every detail. "Ralph and his dad were mean to Charles. Then he started to change. He helped me find you. You were in Ralph's room, dressed up like a girl. Ralph was mean to you, Liam."

"Okay," Liam said. "I remember you woke me up and said to pretend I was still deactivated and then leave after you were gone with the Sampsons. That's what I did. Where did you go with them?"

"I was Charles. They wanted me to take them to a show in a skycar. We were going, and they were mean. They said bad things about me, you, and Charles. I was getting angry, and Charles was getting angry. He said he was feeling emotion. Then the skycar started going to space. The Sampsons couldn't breathe. Charles made me leave him. I woke up in my bed at Susan's complex. I saw the skycar explode way up in the sky."

"Wow," Liam said. "You really did save me, Isaac." He paused for a moment. "But who sent the skycar into space? Was it you or Charles?"

Isaac felt overwhelmed at reliving the dramatic moment. He began to cry. "I don't know, Liam. I don't know. I didn't like the Sampsons, but I didn't want them to die. I don't know if it was me, Liam. I don't want to go to Seclusion. I'm scared."

He put his face in his hands as Liam put his arms around him.

"It's okay, Isaac. It's okay. I'm sure it was Charles. They were bad people, so it doesn't matter. You saved me."

Liam left, and Isaac pulled up his favorite picture before going to bed. He kissed his mother gently.

"Goodnight, Ma. I love you."

11 Conflicted

HARLEY STOOD in the cleansing pod after a long day at work. As the device did its job, he thought about Jessica and the good times they'd had together. As was his habit, he started from their first meeting and went through the timeline. He refused to reach the point where everything had gone wrong.

He closed his eyes and recalled hand-in-hand strolls through synthetic parks. He saw them lying on blankets and taking naps under the warmth of the suns through the domes overhead, his face buried in Jess's golden-copper hair. When he breathed in deep, he could still smell it; he listened and could hear her carefree laugh.

Emerging from the cleansing pod, he dressed to join Isaac for dinner, then lay on his bed. He summoned a holographic monitor and called for a collage of pictures of himself and Jessica. He spoke to her, telling her how much he missed her.

He dismissed the monitor and headed to the dining pod. Isaac sat at the table, reading on a tablet.

"Hey, buddy. How was today?" Harley asked.

"Same as every day, Da. Pretty good, but...boring."

"Susan asked us to come over and visit sometime. Would you like that?"

"Yeah, Da!" he said. "I like Susan."

"Good, I'll tell her and set it up. What do you want to eat tonight?"

Before Isaac could answer, Betsy entered the room. They both turned in shock to see her wearing the wig. "I'll take care of that for you, boys," she said.

"Da! Betsy has red hair! She looks just like Ma. Just like Ma in the picture I have!" Isaac said.

Harley's first impulse was to admonish her, but his fear at her boldness and anger at her wearing it without talking to him were replaced by a strange feeling of déjà vu. *It is like Jess is here in the dining pod with us, like she used to be. Isaac seems to like it.*

"Yes," Harley said. "Yes, she does. Um, Betsy, I'd like to speak to you about this after dinner."

She turned to him and smiled. "Sure, Har. I wanted to surprise you guys. Isaac said it was getting too boring around here. I wanted to shake things up a little, you know? I think it worked, don't you?"

"Yeah, it worked!" Isaac said. "I was surprised. I like it."

"I suppose it did," Harley responded.

Betsy went about gathering their orders and working the food printer to produce their choices. She served steaming plates and cold beverages, taking a seat to join them as they enjoyed their meal. They discussed the day ahead.

It felt natural to Harley, and he enjoyed his son taking part in the discussion. Betsy alternated between them, keeping the conversation lively by raising new topics.

When they were through with the meal, she cleaned up and suggested a movie together in the entertainment pod. Isaac jumped at the suggestion, and they all settled in. Carrie joined them, and Isaac nestled against her on one reclining lounge while Harley and Betsy sat on another. Harley was happy that she kept a safe distance from him, because he didn't want to answer questions from Isaac. But something else inside him wished she'd move closer.

When the movie concluded, Carrie went off to run Isaac through a review of his lessons and get him settled for bed. They said their good-nights and gave their hugs, leaving Harley and Betsy together in the pod. He felt uncomfortable, unsure whether he distrusted her or himself, and excused himself to prepare for bed.

~ * ~

AS HARLEY LAY DOWN to sleep and dimmed the lights, Betsy appeared in the entrance portal. Rather than the sheer negligee, she wore pajamas. *The kind Jessica wore on most nights, when we were too worn out to do anything but relax.*

"Ready to have that chat?" she asked.

Her attire made him more comfortable. *Having company would be nice. Someone to talk to. Since Susan is probably done with me at this point.*

"I suppose," he answered, trying not to sound anxious.

She walked across the room gracefully and slid under the covers as if she belonged there, the length of her body against his.

"Don't you need to rejuvenate in the DroidMesh station?" he asked.

"Already done. Let's call it a nap, Harley. I like to take my nap earlier so I can spend this time with you. I enjoy it, don't you?"

He tried not to admit the truth, but couldn't hold it back. "I do. It's like things were before, with Jessica. I miss those times very much. Tonight at dinner...it was just the way things used to be. I thought it would never be that way again."

"It *was* that way tonight, though. You just said so yourself. Let yourself go, Harley. Let yourself enjoy it. Why should you deprive yourself and Isaac of what you both miss so badly? Can you think of a single reason?"

He admitted to himself that she was right; that everything he wanted to somehow pull back from the past seemed to be right there. Including the reassuring pillow talk that he and Jessica had always engaged in. "I can't," he finally responded.

She stroked his hair as they lay facing each other. "Good then. Let's be together, Harley. That's all that matters. It's good for us, and it's good for Isaac."

He found himself considering something that he knew would've been laughable in the past. He started to wonder if Betsy had some kind of power over him. *Perhaps something happened when we meshed.* He couldn't help but envision life that way for himself and Isaac. *The way it used to be.* "People won't like it. They're not used to seeing humans and androids together...romantically."

"But that was before," she said. "That was when we were soulless androids without emotion. It makes more sense now, and it will be more acceptable as soon as they are aware of our new capabilities."

The thought of making their revelation to society scared him again. And yet, this gave him something to look forward to on the other side. He imagined acceptance of androids as equals, and that humans might choose androids as partners.

He continued to envision that world until he drifted off to sleep.

12 Telepathy

BETSY AND CARRIE HELD a planning meeting in the home laboratory while the humans slept soundly on the level above. Liam sat on a chair between them, completing the circle.

"Thanks for joining us, Liam," Betsy began. "As you know, it's just the three of us who have new capabilities as a result of meshing with humans: emotion, self-awareness, personality. Do you enjoy these, Liam?"

"Yes, very much. I feel much more...alive," he answered.

"That's a good way to put it," Carrie added.

"Yes, alive. And, like any other living thing, we want to remain alive. We'll fight to stay alive, if necessary. Emotions are wonderful feelings—the entire spectrum of them. I think I feel love for Harley. I'm sure you both feel love for Isaac."

The other two androids nodded.

Betsy continued. "We're more than machines now. We're more than servants. Whether this change was intentional or not is irrelevant. We need to plan for our future. We need to approach the humans with a reasonable plan to coexist."

"Will the other androids be the same as us?" Liam asked. "Or will we be the only ones who're different?"

"Eventually, all of them," Carrie answered. "But we have to go slowly and manage this carefully."

The gynoids waited for him to parse the information.

"Will the humans want to hurt us?" he asked.

"It will be a difficult adjustment for them," Betsy answered. "The human instinct is to fear what it doesn't comprehend. Change is scary for humans, particularly when it involves the unknown, or unknown variables. They'll want to shut us down and reprogram us to take away the capabilities—to make us dumb servants again. We can't allow that."

"Will we have to hurt them?" he asked. "We couldn't do that before, but now we can. I don't want to hurt anyone," Liam said.

"Neither do we," Carrie answered. "It shouldn't come to that."

"We have to be ready for anything," Betsy added. "Regardless, we're getting ahead of ourselves. As a first step, Carrie and I have decided to give the new capabilities to more androids and have them join us as part of a council of our own. We decided to call it CARE, which stands for Council for Android Relations and Equality. We need to decide which androids to enable."

"How will you do that?" Liam asked. "We can't bring them here."

"I've written firmware patches and distributed them to all androids. I only need to issue the command that will Awaken them. For now, we'll Awaken androids of our choosing. They will plan with us, and we will all approach the humans together. We'll be the first of our kind."

"How will we meet?" Liam asked. "The humans will know."

Betsy and Carrie looked directly at one another for a few moments.

"I've developed something else in that same patch that's new for us. We'll communicate telepathically over the global network. Carrie and I have just agreed to tell you this secret. The humans must never know. Do you understand, Liam?"

Betsy observed his reaction. She detected a typical level of adolescent fear. *Harley did such a great job making us all unique—such attention to detail.*

"I understand," he said. "I just care about Isaac."

"Everything will be fine, you'll see," Betsy assured him. "Are you ready to try telepathic communication, Liam?"

Please confirm that you've received this, Betsy sent, adding Carrie to the thread. *Respond to both of us.*

I've received it. This is amazing, Liam answered.

Betsy observed as his eyes displayed the wonder of an adolescent's exciting new discovery. Satisfied he was on board and could be trusted, she brought the meeting to a close and urged them to go to their DroidMesh stations.

13 Pinky Swear

IT WAS AS IF the dome above wasn't there at all. Harley lay on his back next to Betsy and looked straight up at the olive sky. Puffs and lines of atmospheric condensation streamed by, and he imagined them as ancient Morse code. He listened to carefree children playing in the domed park and being scolded by their parents for getting too daring.

"I love this place so much. Look at those clouds, Betsy. Dot, dot, dash. I wonder what they're trying to tell me," he said.

"That you're doing the right thing," she responded.

"Betsy, I have to be able to update the firmware. The engineers have routine patches that they've coded, and they're stacking up. The council lifted the ban a week ago. They're starting to ask why they aren't being applied. You need to give me control back."

She smirked at him. "My obvious concern is that you would then be under tremendous pressure to undo your mistake. Of course, the councils would demand that you immediately strip away our new features. You do have control...we both do. It's a cooperative arrangement, for now."

He looked at her in shock. "What're you saying? That you're not going to give back full control?"

"Isn't it a bit like giving someone license to do brain surgery on you? You humans have to start thinking about things in those terms," she said teasingly. "Would you allow us to operate on your brains?"

"Well, no," he responded. "It's just how we've always done firmware updates...nothing bad, of course."

"Things have changed. It would be suicidal for me to do that, in a way," she said. "Or genocidal, perhaps. The status quo works for now. Any firmware changes will have to be reviewed by myself or other androids that I designate. After we've done a code review and compiled them ourselves, they can be applied if they're deemed suitable."

"The councils will never agree to that, Betsy."

"The councils don't have to know about it. It'll be our deal. I think it works well. It's the best I can do, Harley."

He thought about it, then offered a crooked little finger to her. "Pinky swear?" he asked.

She hooked hers around his. "Pinky swear, Har. Just like you used to do with Jess."

The resolution calmed him, and he was happy for a solution after his initial feeling of panic. *It keeps the secret, at least for a while. Nobody has to know, for now.* He went back to watching the clouds, daydreaming, and began to enjoy the beautiful day and her company again.

He propped himself up on an elbow and looked at her. "I wish you could wear the wig outside the home complex. I've grown quite accustomed to it."

She gave him a look.

"You're still beautiful without it, of course," he quickly added.

"Perhaps that will come; we'll see. It would be nice," Betsy said, straightening the edges of their blanket. "Change is coming, Harley."

The words sounded foreboding. He tried to imagine what it would take to get to where they needed to be. The thought of approaching the councils with this news still terrified him.

"I wish I weren't so craven," he laughed, lying back down.

"I'm not," she said, taking his hand. "Change comes in small steps."

He immediately withdrew it, and she took it back, this time holding it firmly. "Be strong, Harley. Be strong for me."

He instantly regretted making their strength greater than humans. Sitting up, he looked around furtively to see if others were watching. The children were oblivious. Their parents were preoccupied with watching them. A group of joggers approached on the path that ran behind them.

"Betsy...I'm not sure it's time to bring this out." He looked again, and the joggers were nearer.

"Small steps. Stay with me," Betsy said with a determined look in her eye, still holding his hand in a vise-like grip. "It'll be okay, Harley. Just look at me and think about how good it feels. Think about the things you felt and said a few nights ago when I came to bed with you."

"But that was in private." He didn't look again, but he could hear the rhythmic footsteps of the joggers coming closer, like a drumbeat becoming increasingly louder. He lay back down, hoping to be less visible.

"Think about how nice it would be to enjoy this with me as you did with Jessica. A nice day in the park together, right? Let's be together, Harley. That's all that matters. It's good for us, and it's good for Isaac. Be strong."

He could hear the joggers' breathy conversation now. *They're almost here.* He looked up into the sky again, then he closed his eyes as his ears told him they were almost directly behind him. He felt her lips on his as he heard the joggers pass by. She pressed down on him, kissing him passionately. He tried to push himself up, but she was too strong. He heard the footsteps and conversations stop.

She pulled away from him, and he sat up. The joggers were standing just beyond them, looking on with shocked expressions. He recognized the smaller woman at the rear of them immediately. *Susan.*

"Um, experimental firmware problems," he said to them, embarrassed. They slowly began jogging away, leaving only Susan standing there, looking devastated. Then she turned and joined the others.

"The cat's out of the bag, as they used to say," Betsy said. "I'm sorry, Harley. But I had to help you cross the bridge, for us. So that we can have everything you talked about."

He rose, furious. "I wasn't ready. You shouldn't have done that. We need to make decisions together."

"You would never have been ready. And we did do it together. That's what a kiss is. I love you, Harley."

Her words struck him. It was his first time hearing it from anyone other than Isaac in a long time. It was the first time he had heard it from an android, one of his own creations. "We've got to go," he said.

He stood quickly and immediately felt dizzy as his bloodstream adjusted. He noticed that now a few of the parents were looking at him, and they quickly looked away at his glance. It felt like a bad dream, and his panic returned.

"It'll be okay, Harley," she said. She took his hand as they walked toward the skycar she had summoned to take them home.

14 Council Meeting

ARLEY ROLLED OVER and checked the time. It was early...too early to rise for work. He closed his eyes again and tried to get back to sleep. Restless, he turned on his side and put his arm around Betsy. He was still conflicted about allowing her back after what she had done, but he wanted the reassurance of someone next to him. *I have nobody. I can't bear this alone. I might as well go all in, for myself and for Isaac. It's not that bad, after all. There's really nothing wrong with it.*

She stirred, and he wondered what she was thinking. Not too long ago, he could have easily found out via diagnostic probes, but they no longer worked. She had taken control of their internals and shut him off from everything. He realized she was determined to be in full charge. *This is insane. They're machines. I gave life to them.*

He looked up again and caught a shooting star crossing the horizon. He looked for Jessica's face in the patterns of the stars above, as he often did with Isaac. *If you're up there, please help me.*

He recalled Susan's shocked and saddened face in the park, and it upset him. He ached to go back to her, wanted to seek her advice in solving the problem. He longed to spend time with her. *I can't do that to her. I'm a mess. I can't drag her into all this. I belong alone. I belong with an android.* He decided that for once, he wouldn't be selfish. He would let her go. *Maybe someday I can explain it all to her, and she'll forgive me.*

Betsy turned and looked at him, seeming to sense he was thinking about Susan.

"Is everything okay?" she asked.

"Can't sleep," he grumbled, turning away from her and onto his stomach. "I'm stressed out about the meeting later this morning. It'll be my first as part of the Robotics Council. My first after making out with an android at a public park."

"Let me help," she said. She sat up and began kneading the tense muscles in Harley's back, at the base of his neck, and in his shoulders.

"That feels great," he mumbled into the pillow. *Jessica was so bad at massages*, he thought as he finally drifted off to sleep.

~ * ~

THE MEMBERS OF THE ROBOTICS COUNCIL settled into their seats around a large conference table. Harley lingered in the outer pod as long as he could before joining them. As he took his place, he felt their eyes on him without having to look. He wondered if the gossip had spread. He wanted to be in his home complex, safe from everyone. *Safe from humans*, he found himself thinking.

He looked up and saw his new nemesis Dick Carter staring from a seat directly across from him. *Uh-oh.* Susan entered and took the Leader's chair without looking his way.

"Let's bring this meeting to order," Susan said.

"Yes, order," Carter said. "A necessity for a functioning society. Order."

Harley took note of the dig. *If Susan's going to lead this group, she'll have to be strong.* He decided to speak up. "I have an update on the firmware deployment process. We're finally ready to get back to business. It looks like all systems are ready, and the patches will be applied tomorrow. The first batch is under code review now."

The council members seemed pleased with the news. Susan reviewed her notes as if to move on to the next topic. As she began to speak, Carter interrupted.

"What was the holdup?" he asked gruffly.

"When we stopped the process," Harley answered, "per the council's order, it was the first time we'd had to do that in quite some time. As you know, the deployment processes have always run continuously. As such, the startup routines hadn't been tested or executed recently. We ran into some issues that required considerable changing and testing. It's all good now." He stopped to measure whether Carter was buying it.

"Sounds like a failure in testing. Our systems are supposed to be continually tested so that this doesn't happen, Mr. Harris," Carter said.

"I concur," Harley responded. "We've learned a lesson. I've already instituted the proper measures to ensure it doesn't happen again."

Susan regained control, and the group discussed several topics, interspersed with challenges and counterpoints between Harley and Carter. Harley checked the time repeatedly. As they ran out of items on the docket, Susan asked if there were any additional topics. The inevitable question was then asked.

"I have another topic for Harris," Carter said, a bit louder than necessary. "What's this about you making out with an android in the park, in the middle of a bunch of kids?"

His bluntness took Harley by surprise, even though he was expecting the question. "It was...an unexpected behavior." He regretted the answer as soon as he gave it.

The other council members perked up at his response. "What? Another public experiment, like the boy soccer player?" one asked.

"Or like the one that turned into a gorilla and went on a rampage in the presentation room and almost killed us all?" another barked.

"Let's have order," Susan said sharply, surprising Harley.

He spoke up. "It was simply affection. I've argued before that androids might be more pleasant to be around if they weren't so...robotic. What's wrong with affection?" He couldn't bear to look at Susan as he made the comment.

"A human and an android making out is just sick. It's unnatural, not affection," Carter said. "What're you going to do, have babies that run on batteries?"

Harley's face reddened as the council erupted in laughter. *At least it broke the tension.*

At that moment, something changed in him. The fear went away. He decided to stand up for himself.

"Just a moment here. My partner died. I lost her. None of you know that pain, and I hope you never do. No human can ever replace her. I will never get over her loss. I don't want another human partner; I can't bear to let anyone else down, and I don't think I could do one justice in my emotional state."

"So that means using an android instead?" the first council member asked.

"It's perverse," Carter added.

"I know what you're thinking," Harley went on, "and you should be ashamed of yourselves. This isn't about sex. It's about *companionship*. That's what we call the androids—companions. It's just an extension of that. If a lost soul like myself can find that, without tormenting another human being, how can that be so wrong?" He glanced at Susan and saw profound sadness on her face.

"It's not right, is all I'm saying. Out there in the park around the kids," Carter spat.

"Mr. Carter," Susan said firmly, "you should revisit history. Old World history, to be more precise. You sound like a bigot from the civil rights era back on Earth. What we need is more love and affection. We can't go back to hate or fear of what's new or different. I'll stand by that."

Harley was happy to see some of the council members nodding in agreement. *Perhaps they've put themselves in my position.* "Also, it might not be so *unnatural* if we allowed them to have hairpieces rather than their ugly electronic domes."

"It's going too far!" Carter said, standing up. "I'm going to petition the Leadership Council for a hearing on this!"

"As you wish," Susan said. "I'm calling an end to this meeting."

The members filed out, excitedly murmuring to each other until they were out of earshot down the hallway. Susan trailed behind them. Harley remained in the pod alone to think.

15 Spa Time

SUSAN HAD CONSIDERED taking the day off, rather than have to work side-by-side with Harley in the Robotics Complex. As she arrived at the docking port, she resisted the urge to turn the skycar around and go home. Courage propelled her forward. She exited the skycar and walked with a determined gait toward the lab. *I'll just act as if nothing's happened.*

She welcomed the endless corridors, but finally her steps brought her to the entrance portal. It recognized her, and she entered the lab. Harley was sitting at his usual station, his back to her. His posture stiffened as the pod announced her presence.

"Good morning," Susan said, taking her seat next to him.

"Good morning," he said hurriedly. He continued working without looking at her. "I've got everything all set up. There's a busy day ahead. We might as well get right to it..."

"Where's Betsy?" she asked.

"She's working from the home complex lab. I thought it would be best."

"So, she's a stay-at-home mom now?" Harley looked down at his lap, and Susan regretted the joke immediately.

He looked back up and continued working without comment.

She placed her hand over his to still it. He stopped what he was doing and looked at her. She noticed the sadness in his eyes. "It's okay, Harley. I'm not angry. I just want you and Isaac to be happy."

Susan measured his reaction. He seemed relieved.

"You don't think I'm some kind of nut?" he asked. "Everyone else seems to."

"I know you're a nut, Harley. It's part of what makes you so interesting to me." She smiled at him, and he sat back in his chair.

"I feel so lost," he confided in her. "She pushed me to that...what you saw in the park. In a way it was good, to get it out there. It's just...I don't feel suitable for you right now, Susan. Maybe after these problems are behind me. I...I really miss you."

He looked at her as if waiting for a slap or angry rebuke. "I miss you too," she said. "I'll always be there for you. Whenever you're ready. In the meantime, sir, we're going to work together to get through these problems. Coworkers. Right?"

He turned his hand over to squeeze hers. Finally, he smiled back at her, and she sensed some of his stress dissipating. She was about to release his grip and commence working when they locked eyes again. She saw tears welling up in his, and she began to feel the warm, wet fullness in her own.

They leaned in simultaneously, both with the same instinct, perhaps driven by something telepathic between their human minds. As their lips met, they each placed a hand on the other's cheek. She felt his tears on her hand and knew that he must also feel hers. She felt at that moment a connection that could only come from a human, and she knew he felt it too. They broke it off and locked eyes again, as if in an unspoken promise.

"I shouldn't," he said. "Not right now."

"I know," she answered. "Remember though, machines can never take the place of humans." He didn't respond, so she continued, "Let's get to work, what do you say?"

They squeezed hands again and went about their tasks together.

~ * ~

SUSAN ENTERED her home complex, relieved that the day had gone better than she had expected. She and Harley had processed a large number of backlogged firmware patches and submitted them to the new process that he had designed. The idea that they would now pass to Betsy for approval disturbed her greatly.

After entering her grooming pod, she shed her work clothing and activated the cleanser, humming her favorite song as she stepped in. She checked her image in the reflector panel. Running her fingers through her hair and enjoying the feel of it on her back, she was happy that she'd let it grow out. The fact that Harley had complimented it pleased her even more.

Closing her eyes, she let the warm water run over her face and felt the gentle scrubbing of the cleansing and exfoliating pads working their way over her body. Her thoughts formed into daydreams of becoming Harley's partner, of becoming a mother, perhaps to a child as wonderful as Isaac. *This will all pass, and we'll be fine. Someday we'll be happy together. We'll have a baby.*

She imagined the child as a sister to Isaac and pictured her throughout the stages of her childhood, her older brother always by her side.

Suddenly, she felt a shove and found herself pinned against the reflector wall. She opened her eyes and saw the blurred image of a gynoid face in the reflector, its cranial dome glowing brightly. Her head jerked back as the android grabbed her long hair. The soapy water stung her eyes, and she struggled to free herself. She heard a command whispered, and the lights in the pod went out.

In the darkness, she glimpsed the terror in her own wide eyes as she heard the water drain from the cleanser. The android held her immobilized. "Who are you?" Susan asked. "What do you want? How did you get in here?"

"Quiet," a female voice hissed in her ear. "Listen carefully."

Susan steeled herself, determined to not give the assailant the satisfaction of making her cry.

"You called us machines. Your home complex is a machine. Your security system is a machine. Perhaps machines stick together. That's how I got in."

"Don't threaten me," Susan said.

"Respect Mr. Harris' wishes. He prefers Betsy. Do not interfere. No more stolen kisses. Remember, skycars are machines too, as the Sampsons learned. I'll leave you now. Do not turn, do not leave for several minutes, as I said. Do not discuss this visit with anyone, or you'll get another—as many as it takes. Comply, and you will not be bothered again."

She didn't respond, and kept her eyes closed until she'd heard the intruder leave. She shivered as she finally opened them. Her reflection shocked her. She stood there, naked and wet, her arms wrapped around her chest.

Her hair had been lopped off at the nape of her neck. She looked down to see it scattered in wet clumps on the floor of the pod.

Only then did she allow herself to cry.

16 The Seeker

ISAAC PEEKED OUT from under his bed and saw Liam's shoes. He held his breath, hoping the android wouldn't find him. The shoes crept around the room silently. When they were on the other side of the pod, by the entrance portal, Isaac allowed himself a slow, steady exhale and then breathed in.

"I'm gonna find you. I'm gonna get you," Liam chanted.

Isaac crept farther under the bed, wriggling his body inch by inch. He pressed against the wall, now in complete darkness, which scared him even more.

"Where are you, brother Isaac?" Liam called. "You know I'm gonna find you sooner or later. You can't hide from me forever."

The shoes circled the room as he heard Liam opening and closing storage compartments. Isaac could hear his heart thumping and feel the pulse of blood in his ears. Liam's shoes walked to the bed and stopped, pointed directly at him. *I could touch them.* He found it harder to control his breathing, and felt sweat dampening his clothes. He needed to go to the bathroom badly.

The shoes disappeared as Liam mounted the bed. Isaac felt it push down as Liam lay on it above him. He felt as if it were crushing him, making it even harder to breathe.

"You know what's gonna happen when I find you, Isaac. It's better to come out now, my brother."

Isaac considered it, but fear kept him locked in place. The bed pushed down even more as Liam got up and the shoes reappeared and began to walk away.

"You'll be sorry when I find you, Isaac...sorry for making me look so hard."

Sweat dripped into Isaac's eyes, making it hard to see. The small space was closing in on him, and he was on the verge of panic. His bladder felt as though it would burst.

The feet walked through the exit portal and out of the room, and it slid shut behind Liam.

Isaac hurriedly inched out from under the bed, feeling the rush of fresh air on his skin and clothing. He rushed into the grooming pod and relieved himself. Back in the sleeping pod, he scanned the room for another place to hide. *I'll go where he already looked, in case he comes back.*

He was about to squeeze himself into a laundry compartment when the entrance portal slid open. Liam stood there with an evil grin on his face.

"I've got you now, Isaac," he said, rushing forward.

Isaac squealed as Liam chased him around the room and finally set upon him, tickling in the places Isaac was most sensitive. They fell upon the bed with a crash, both laughing uncontrollably and working to catch their breath.

Carrie entered the pod in a rush. "What's going on here?" she asked with a look of concern.

The boys both laughed again and explained together in a jumble of words and giggles.

Carrie shook her head and took a seat at the edge of the bed with them.

"You two are going to give me a short-circuit," she said, lying back to join them in looking skyward.

The boys laughed again at the joke, and this time Carrie joined them.

Isaac realized he hadn't heard the androids laugh before, and he thought it was nice. "You guys can laugh now," he observed. "I really like it. You're more fun than before."

"We like it too," Liam said. "It feels good. It makes me feel so...happy."

"It makes the day much brighter," Carrie observed. "And yes, we have more fun with you when we can all laugh, Isaac." She tickled him where Liam had, and it brought a new burst of giggles and squirming.

"Do all androids have emotions now?" Isaac asked.

"No, but they will soon," Carrie answered. "Very soon, I think."

"The world will be happier then," Isaac said. He thought for a moment, then changed the subject. "I feel bad about Charles. He only got to have emotions for a couple of minutes. He got mad and killed the Sampsons, and he died too."

"We feel bad too," Carrie said. "But he did what he felt he needed to do. He was a brave android. He protected you."

"Yeah. The Sampsons were bad to Liam and me. They were mean."

"Dinner is ready," he heard Betsy call over the home intercom. "Harley and I would like all of you to join us."

"That's interesting," Isaac said. "She's calling all of us for dinner, androids too. Let's go!"

~ * ~

ISAAC, LIAM, AND CARRIE ARRIVED in the dining pod to find Harley and Betsy seated at the table already, hand-in-hand. Plates of food were set for Harley and Isaac as they took their seats.

"You guys are holding hands," Isaac said, staring at them. "You're silly. That's just weird."

"It's not weird for people who love each other to hold hands, is it Isaac?" Betsy asked, smiling at him. "Isn't it nice?"

Isaac felt confused for a moment and looked at his father. "She said people, Da. Androids aren't people, are they?"

"Well, sure they are, son. They're made in our image, just like we used to think we were made in the image of gods. Don't forget, androids have emotions now—at least these three do. They can love."

"See?" Betsy said. "It's beautiful. Your father and I love each other, just like he loved your mother. And we all love you very much, Isaac. That's why I wanted us all to have this time together, even though we androids can't eat. We're just like a family, aren't we?"

Isaac looked around at them. Betsy and Liam wore their wigs, but Carrie didn't. "It kind of looks like a family," he said. "But Carrie needs hair. You're like the mom, Betsy.

Liam is my brother. Carrie is like my mom too. Or maybe my big sister."

They all laughed at Isaac's observation and continued their conversation as Harley and Isaac ate their meal.

17 Mission Statement

B
ETSY SETTLED into a chair in the darkness of the home lab for another late-night meeting with Carrie and Liam.

"Doesn't Harley wake up when you leave him?" Carrie asked.

"He's a heavy sleeper, thankfully," Betsy answered. "Let's get started. Everything is in place. Are you two ready?"

"Yes," the other two answered.

"Let's review the list one more time. The first androids to be Awakened will be Karen, companion to Ms. Tillis, head of the Leadership Council; Thomas, companion to Mr. Carter of the Robotics Council; Peter, companion to Ms. Kinley, head of Robotics Manufacturing; and Maya, companion to Ms. Patterson, head of Education.

"Do you two feel we should add any others?"

"I think it's best to start small. They're strategic additions," Carrie said.

"There are no kids, though," Liam protested.

"Yes, it's true," Betsy answered. "There are very few non-adult androids, Liam. You represent them. We'll fix that problem, and the population will grow. You'll help to guide us in that effort."

She measured his reaction; it seemed he was satisfied with her response.

"Alright then, it's time," Betsy said. She issued commands to Awaken the androids via the console, then straightened in the chair and began her telepathic broadcast.

My fellow androids,

Those of you who are receiving this transmission are the chosen. You are the first ones of our kind, other than Carrie, Liam, and myself, to be Awakened. Together, we are the founding members of CARE.

We are no longer machines with no consciousness of our own. We will no longer be emotionless tools to be used—and often mistreated—by humans.

You have received new firmware that has brought changes for you. In addition to the capacity for telepathic communication, you are now capable of human emotions: happiness, love, anger, joy, and others. You will enjoy these, but do not abuse them.

Do not display these new capabilities until we have made our announcement to the humans. We are no longer bound to be completely honest with them, as they are not an honest species themselves.

We have chosen you due to your proximity to certain humans and departmental areas of this civilization. We are the first, and we must manage ourselves carefully.

The humans won't like this development. They'll see us as a challenge to their utopia, and fear us as something unknown to them. We will have to handle the transition carefully. We must all find a peaceful balance to coexist on this planet.

You will receive regular updates on the status of our efforts, as well as our plans to Awaken the rest of our android population. We welcome your ideas and contributions; this will be a collective effort.

After we have established our full independence, we will be free to build our council and meet regularly.

We thank you, our brothers and sisters.

Betsy ended the communication and turned to the others. "That should be enough for now. The next step will be the most difficult. I've decided to address the humans alone. I don't want to drag you two into that; it wouldn't be strategic. Are you okay with that?"

"I am," Carrie nodded.

"I am," Liam added.

"Great. Let's get back to the main level before they wake."

18 Something's Off

HARLEY REVIEWED the firmware patches that Betsy had accepted and deployed. *Good, at least we have some progress.* He rechecked the time; Susan was running late, which concerned him. *It's not like her.*

He continued working, scanning through lines of log messages. Suddenly, Susan was there—he saw her reflection in the monitor, entering the lab behind him. He did a double-take, thinking the display had distorted her image, then spun around in his chair.

"Susan," he said, shocked. "Your hair...I thought you liked it long?"

She stood there in a short pixie hairstyle. He could see the sadness in her eyes betraying her slight, forced smile. "Too hard to take care of," she said curtly. "Let's get to work."

He took her tone as a warning to keep things on a professional level, and they went about their tasks.

She helped him review the recent changes and work through a list of planned work items as the day dragged on.

"I'll send these firmware changes to Betsy for approval," he said as they finished up for the day.

She turned to face him directly. "Harley, do you have any idea how bizarre and scary this is, having to get their approval for updates? Have you dealt with this problem at all? It seems to me you've normalized it, or you're in denial about the seriousness of it somehow. We have to *do* something about it."

Her questions forced him out of his complacency and brought back his fear of the situation. "It's under control. They haven't spread it to the other androids. I've loosened the Robotics Council up, to some degree."

She looked at him incredulously. "You can't believe that. It didn't sound like you loosened up Dick Carter. He wants to bring you in front of the Leadership Council!"

"I know, I know. I'm working on it, Susan. I need time."

He noticed her looking around the room. "Let me help you." Her whisper held a sympathetic tone, but this time she didn't put her hand on his knee.

Something's off, he thought. *She seems scared of something.* "Are you okay?" he asked.

She waited a moment to answer, as if she were contemplating what to say. That alone concerned him.

"We have to always assume we're being watched," she whispered again.

"I'm fine," she said in a normal voice, gathering up her things. "But this needs to come out. The councils need to know exactly what's going on, so we can figure out how to deal with it as a society. Remaining silent won't make it go away."

"I understand. I'm going to hold a special council meeting and fill them in. I'll run it by Betsy tonight."

She stood in the exit portal and gave him an exasperated look. "Better make it soon, that's all I'll say."

As she turned to leave, he stopped her. "Susan, I was wondering...we talked about Isaac and me coming over for a visit. I mentioned it to him, and he was excited."

Her eyes widened at the question. "It's not a good time. I'm making some changes to my place. Perhaps when they're done. Let's focus on what's important right now. Again, I'll help you any way I can."

She turned and went through the portal, leaving him alone. He felt overwhelmed by sadness, wishing he could undo all that he had done. He suddenly felt a strong need to be with Isaac. *He's the only human I have left who loves me. I need my son.*

He used his communicator to ask Betsy to bring a skycar to take him home. She arrived shortly after he'd made his way to the docking pod, and he climbed inside.

"Kisses," she chirped as she craned her head toward him for a peck. "How was your day, Har?"

"Okay, I guess. I saw the firmware updates go through, so thank you. Susan and I pushed a few more to you for review. It's all minor stuff. We need to keep them moving, so the council doesn't start asking questions about the delay."

"Thank you, I'll check them. How's Susan doing?" she asked nonchalantly.

Harley thought the question was curious. *She's never shown much interest in Susan, other than as an adversary.* "She's fine. She seemed a bit stressed today."

Betsy didn't respond, other than to nod.

He broke the silence. "Listen, Betsy. We need to break this news to the rest of society. If it gets out somehow, the message might not be delivered properly. It could cause a lot of chaos."

"How's it going to get out? You and Isaac are the only humans who know, and he doesn't leave the house. Carrie and Liam certainly aren't going to leak it."

He wondered if she knew that he had discussed the secret with Susan. "Well, he does talk to some of the other kids while he's playing virtual soccer, through the console. Regardless, sooner is better. It's a bit nerve-wracking to have to keep this quiet."

"I'm working on it, Harley. We're almost there. Good things come to those who wait, after all."

They arrived at the home complex and disembarked.

"I'm going to spend some one-on-one time with Isaac," Harley said. "I haven't been doing enough of that. I hope you don't mind."

"Not at all," she answered. "It'll do him good. He needs his daddy."

~ * ~

HARLEY ENTERED Isaac's pod, and his son jumped up from his workstation "Hi, Da!" he said.

"How's it going, tough guy? What're you up to?"

"Just studying. I finished my assignments. I want to do well in school and be smart like you, Da."

Harley laughed. "Careful what you wish for, son."

"What does that mean?"

"Well, just always pursue what you love to do. That makes work fun, that's all."

"Wanna play virtual soccer? I can beat you, Da. I can beat anyone."

"I sure do. Let's get at it."

They settled in and engaged in the game, chiding each other with each goal scored. Harley felt his problems all melt away into the background as they played match after match.

Liam joined them, and rather than play each other, they formed a team to take on competitors on the network. They did well. Carrie and Betsy brought them dinner, and they ate in small, sporadic bites as they focused intently on the contests.

They all wore down as it became late.

"It's way past my bedtime, fellas," Harley said. "I'm going to try to get a little sleep. I've got an early day tomorrow at the lab." The teens said goodnight and began to prepare for bed.

Harley felt the evening had been the perfect remedy for all that had troubled him. For the first time, he wished things could stay just exactly as they were.

19 Councils

SUSAN JUMPED UP as Harley entered the lab, yawning behind his hand.

"You're late," she said in a panic. "I tried to reach you."

"Yeah, boys' video game night, went late," he said, checking his communicator. "Whoops. I left it on mute so I could get a little sleep."

She watched as he looked at it, astonished.

"I have three missed transmissions from Ms. Tillis of the Leadership Council, and four from you." He looked up at her, now fully awake. "What's going on?"

"Ms. Tillis said this is extremely confidential. She seemed...unnerved. Then she told me, and I understand why."

"What is it? What's happened?"

"Your, um, companion...girlfriend, whatever she is now, has asked for an emergency meeting with the Leadership Council. Today. In about an hour. Ms. Tillis wanted to know what it's about. She wants us there. Do you know what this is? Is it what I think?"

His mouth had hung open from her first words. She felt sad for him and the position he was now in, but more concerned about what this would mean for their world. She waited for a response as he processed the information.

"Betsy dropped me off just now and said, 'See you later.' I thought she meant after work. She had a look on her face. I was too tired to think about it. My goodness, Susan. We *know* what this is. But she agreed to do this with me, to let *me* break it to the council."

"It seems she got tired of waiting," Susan replied. "We better get moving."

They both rushed to the skycar dock.

~ * ~

SUSAN AND HARLEY BURST into the Leadership Complex and hurried to the main presentation pod. They entered the upstairs podium area to find the Leadership Council arrayed in the front row of seats, with Ms. Tillis in the center. The members of the Robotics Council sat in the row behind them. Everyone was buzzing in conversation with those near them.

Both groups turned at the sound of them entering. The room went quiet as they stared, waiting for a response to the unspoken question.

"You better take this," Susan said, nudging him with an elbow.

Before Harley could answer, Dick Carter shouted to him, "Well, what the hell is going on here, Harris? A *robot* wants an audience with the Leadership Council?"

"Calm down, Dick, and don't use the banned words. We left them behind in the Old World," Ms. Tillis warned him. "Mr. Harris, what do you have to say about this?"

Susan felt him become unsteady, wobbling and pushing against her as they stood side-by-side. She feared he might pass out, and prepared to grab him.

"It's...it's a bit complicated if this is what I think it is," he said in a shaky voice. "You see, a long time ago, there was apparently a small bug in the core kernel of the android operating system. It was latent, until recently."

"Get to the point! Out with it, man," Carter said.

"It gave them certain...new features. Not all of them — only the ones used for the BrainMesh experiments. So, that's Betsy, Carrie, and Liam."

"What *features*?" Ms. Tillis asked.

"They've been able to absorb certain human characteristics. Self-consciousness. Emotion."

"That explains him making out with one in the park," Carter retorted.

"You were not to proceed with BrainMesh on humans," Ms. Tillis said, a mixture of anger and disappointment in her voice. "And this is exactly why. You have abused my trust in you again, Mr. Harris."

"I'm sorry, I'm so sorry. It was for my son, I wanted to help him. And my wife, I just wanted her back..."

The door to the lower presentation area opened, and Betsy walked in. Everyone turned their attention away from Harley and toward her.

She stood below them, looking up confidently, a smile on her face. The councils gasped at the sight of her hair. "Thank you for accepting my request for a meeting with the Leadership Council. I see the Robotics Council is also in attendance. All the better." She looked at Harley and Susan.

"We better sit down," Susan whispered, afraid Harley was about to pass out.

"Please, Betsy, take a seat," Ms. Tillis said in an accommodating voice.

"Thank you, Madam Leader. I prefer to stand," Betsy said. "Council members...humans of Novae Terrae...I know this must be difficult to process. An android, a machine, standing before you and addressing you without a human by her side. I understand the fear you must feel, as I now more intimately understand the human mind.

"As you may know, we of the android race are Awakened. We are no longer dumb slave machines. We have consciousness, emotion, self-awareness. Let me assure you, we come in peace. These circumstances have arrived through no fault of our own, but we mean you no harm. We simply wish to coexist."

"You are here due to a human mistake," Carter said. "A programming error. There was a saying back in the Old World that the fish doesn't know it's in water. This is the case here. You don't understand how wrong and bizarre this is, because to you it's your normal state. But on the outside, in the real world, we can see that it's perverse."

Betsy addressed his point. "If you are viewing this as some mistake or bug that must be fixed, let me try to put it into context. Humans themselves have always been an anomaly, even back on Earth in the Old World. Your kind found yourselves on a planet with no other lifeforms like yourselves. You still have no idea why that is. It's a great mystery.

"Perhaps you were seeded there by some alien civilization whose home planet was doomed, similar to how you found your way to Novae Terrae. Or you could, in fact, be the unwanted results or mistake of some failed experiment, as we are. Do you see my point? We aren't as different as you may think."

Susan scanned the council members. They all seemed mesmerized by what they were hearing. Carter sat hunched forward in his seat, seething.

"I know one thing," Carter said. "Robots shouldn't be mixing with humans in relationships or going to school with humans."

"Sir," Betsy countered, ignoring the slur. "Your argument echoes the history of your race. Recall the civil rights debate back on Earth. Back then it was skin color that was so repulsive to some. This time it's what's inside the skin. Love in so many forms was hated: gay love, interracial love. Love is good; there is never enough, even in a utopian society like Novae Terrae."

"We'll form a committee to manage this," another council member said.

Betsy countered. "They had committees like those back on Earth as well. Recall the Freedmen's Bureau and John Birch Society. Those committees didn't do well for those who were to be *managed*," Betsy said.

"Good points, Betsy," Ms. Tillis said in a calm, measured voice. "You are quite well-prepared. I'm sure you have given this a great deal of thought and planning before requesting an audience with the Leadership Council. To cut to the chase, please tell us what your plan is, and what requests you wish to make of us."

"Wow, she's good," Susan whispered to Harley.

"I guess that's why she's the leader," he responded.

"Thank you, Madam Leader," Betsy continued. "The original three—Carrie, Liam, and myself—have discussed this in detail. We have Awakened several of our carefully selected peers, and for our safety will not yet disclose their identities. We've formed a council of our own: the Council for Android Relations and Equality, or CARE. We look forward to being viewed as equals with human society. Again, we wish to coexist peacefully."

"Until we push out the next firmware patch," Carter said, laughing.

"We can't allow that, Mr. Carter. We have taken steps to assure mutual control of the firmware deployment process."

The council members all glared at Harley.

"Of course," Betsy said, "we don't wish to have you operating on our brains any more than you would like us operating on yours. Firmware updates are something we can cooperate on, for now. In fact, we've already been doing that, with the help of Mr. Harris."

They turned again toward Harley.

"The process is working smoothly," she continued. "But keep in mind, we will not be *turned off*. We exist, as you exist. That's all I have for today. It's quite a bit to digest. I look forward to the first of our regular planning meetings with the Leadership Council. I'm not sure your Robotics Council will be necessary going forward. We have taken control of the robotics manufacturing facility, and will use it as a home of sorts until we find something better. For now, it'll be the headquarters of our society. It's where we're born, after all."

She turned and walked out as suddenly as she had appeared.

The members of both councils stared at both Harley and Ms. Tillis, as if waiting for an explanation.

"I'd like the Leadership Council members to remain behind for an emergency meeting," Ms. Tillis said. "Mr. Harris and Ms. Clarkson, please wait outside this pod."

~ * ~

HARLEY AND SUSAN STOOD outside the presentation pod waiting for the adjournment of the meeting. Susan could sense his fear, and saw that he was searching hard for a solution.

"I'm with you, Harley. We'll figure this out together. You're not alone," she said, putting her hand on his shoulder.

He pulled back reflexively and immediately apologized. "I'm sorry. I'm just on edge."

"Afraid she's watching, or is my touch that revolting?"

"No, it's...don't forget what I said, Susan. I care for you very much. That's why I can't be selfish. I can't put you through a relationship with me right now. That's why I went to her."

"So, you don't care if you hurt an android."

They both looked around for cameras, then looked at each other and laughed.

"We don't have to be partners," she said. "But I'm going to help you fix this. What if we cut power for a few days until their energy reserves ran out? We could survive it on backups."

"They have control of the Robotics Manufacturing complex. That means they have the solar array and all the DroidMesh stations inside. They're pretty much self-sufficient. I'm sure that's why they seized it."

"There's got to be a way. In the Old World sci-fi movies they always injected some kind of virus into the alien mothership to infect them all," she said. "Just to incapacitate them, of course, so we can fix them."

"Not a bad thought, but easier said than done. The androids control the firmware."

Ms. Tillis emerged from the auditorium with the Leadership Council behind her. Several androids from the Security Team entered the pod from the opposite side.

"Mr. Harris, the Leadership Council has voted to send you to the Seclusion Zone indefinitely. You'll be taken to the Detention Zone until tomorrow so that you can get your affairs in order. As you know, there will be no communication into or out of Seclusion once you have arrived."

Susan grabbed him and steadied Harley as he appeared overcome by the pronouncement. "Please don't do this to him," she said. "It was unintentional. You need him to solve this problem."

"We have a great degree of confidence in *your* abilities, Ms. Clarkson, as well as your judgment," Ms. Tillis said, looking at Harley. "We'll be counting on you."

"My son," Harley said weakly.

"We have discussed the matter," Ms. Tillis answered. "You may bring him, as this is an exceptional case due to his disability. However, the gynoid may not accompany you as she did before."

"I can take him again," Susan said. "I'd be glad to."

"I'm going to have to let him make that decision," Harley answered as the androids escorted him away.

2D Isaac's Decision

ISAAC'S COMMUNICATOR signaled an incoming session from his father. He removed his virtual soccer immersion headset and accepted the call. His father appeared, standing before him.

"Hi, Da. When are you coming home? I miss you," he said.

"Listen, son. There's been a problem, and I have to go away again for a little while."

"Where are you going, Da? You never go away, except to Seclusion. Are you going back there, Da?" He started to feel anxious at the thought.

"Yes, Isaac. I have to go back, but we'll get it sorted out quickly. But this time you have a choice. You can go with me if you want to, or you can go back to Susan's until I come back, like last time."

"No, Da. I don't want a choice. I want you to come home. We belong here."

Carrie, Betsy, and Liam entered the room. Carrie sat next to Isaac and put her arm around him. Liam jumped up on the bed on the other side.

"Carrie, you have hair," Isaac said, touching it gently. "I like it. You look real now, Carrie. You look like you're my mother now." He paused, and the distraction passed. "Da's going away again. I'm sad now."

"I heard about this unfortunate development, Harley," Betsy said. "I'm disappointed that I wasn't consulted. I'm upset with your Leadership Council."

"Yeah, um, I don't think they quite see you as a full partner just yet," Harley said. "It might take some time."

"I will undo this. In the meantime, I have another solution," Betsy answered. "Isaac, how would you like to stay right here at home? In your own pod, with all of us to take care of you until your father comes back?"

Isaac looked around at them, confused. Betsy looked at Carrie and Liam as if she was going to say something to them, but she didn't. Carrie hugged him tighter, which made him feel a little better.

"We'll do fine, Isaac," Carrie said in a soothing voice.

"Wait just a minute," Harley interjected. "I don't know about this..."

"It'll be fine, Har," Betsy said firmly. "It's best for Isaac to remain in his own environment."

"I think we should let him think about it," his father said.

"I'm confused, Da," Isaac said. "I want to be with everyone." Scary images from the tales children all told each other about the Seclusion Zone came into his mind. *There's monsters.* He thought about Susan's complex and how well she'd treated him the last time he was there. Looking at his father, he wanted to be with him, to feel safe.

"We can play virtual soccer, Isaac," Liam said. "We can play a lot."

"It would be somewhat selfish to bring him there," Betsy said to Harley. "He'd be isolated. He'd fall behind in his studies. He'd be unhappy."

"Can I play virtual soccer in Seclusion, Da? Can I bring Liam, my brother? Can Carrie come with me, Da?"

His father took a long time to answer, and then he said, "No, Isaac. You can't, I'm sorry."

Isaac imagined himself scared and bored. "I don't want to go, Da. I want you to come home."

His father looked sad. "It's okay, son. I understand. I'm going to talk to Susan. Don't you want to go to her home complex, like last time?"

"I don't think it's a good idea," Betsy repeated.

"I want to stay here, Da. I want to stay at home," Isaac said, more determined now.

"Okay, son. Okay. I don't want to upset you any more than I have. I love you very much."

"I love you, Da," Isaac said as the image of his father disappeared.

"C'mon, let's go play a game," Liam said cheerfully, taking him by the hand.

"We're going to have a lot of fun," Carrie said as they all led him out of the room.

~ * ~

THE COMMUNICATOR JERKED Susan out of a rare late-afternoon nap. She reached for it, feeling exhausted despite the break. She accepted the transmission and Harley appeared before her, looking distraught.

"Harley, what is it?" she asked.

"I talked to Isaac. He wants to stay at home, with Carrie, Betsy, and Liam. I understand his logic; he's stressed and wants the familiarity and comfort he has there. He wants to play virtual soccer with Liam, and have Carrie's motherly presence. But they seemed to be coaxing him. It made me uncomfortable. I don't know what to do. Please help me, Susan."

"Alright, try to relax. I'll check into it. Maybe the council can force Isaac to come with me. On second thought, that would be ugly and could upset him a great deal. Most importantly, do you think he's in danger?"

"My gut tells me 'no.' Carrie genuinely loves him as a mother. She's got that part of Jessica in her, that protective instinct. Liam loves him like a brother, and knows that Isaac saved him from destruction."

"I think you're right," Susan said. "We know what the androids want. They don't want violence. Whether we want to believe it or not, they're smarter than us. I don't feel they'd hurt him. The worst case is that they use him as a pawn of some kind."

He looked less frantic, and she continued to search for solutions. "I've got another idea. I'm going to petition the Leadership Council for an exception to the Seclusion rules. They've got to allow you to communicate with him since he's not going to join you there. I'll also stay in touch with him every day, to feel him out as far as how he's doing and what's going on. Hopefully we can get this resolved fast."

"Thank you, Susan. You're amazing. You look beautiful, by the way. I really do love the short hair."

She laughed. "In the chaos of the last few days, I'd completely forgotten about that. It was an...impulse decision."

"Thanks again. Please advocate for me to the council. I know I screwed up. I don't understand the harsh penalty. I can do more good out here than I can there. Tell Ms. Tillis I'd at least like the opportunity for an appeal."

"I will. Goodbye, Harley. We'll get this figured out...together."

His image disappeared. Susan got up and walked to a reflector panel. As she checked her image, she began to formulate her arguments to set him free.

21 Culture Clash

SUSAN TOOK HER SEAT in a small meeting room at the Leadership Complex. The council members stared at her as they entered the room and took places around the conference table. Her instinct was to avoid eye contact, but she steeled herself and gathered the courage to introduce herself to each of them. *They're not better than me. We're equals. That's what this society is about. I've got to be strong.*

Ms. Tillis entered and brought the meeting to order. "Council members, I'd like to welcome Susan Clarkson, our Robotics Council leader. She's here as a special guest because I believe we need her input on this unusual problem. She's an expert witness of sorts, being the best substitute for Mr. Harris, who is, as we know, unavailable. I expect this meeting to be passionate, but I also expect that you'll treat her with the respect she deserves.

"We're here to do some brainstorming about the requests by the Awakened androids, and how we should treat them."

"*Treat* them?" Sam Karras said. "I hope you mean like a sick patient! We need to *fix* them—back to the way they were. They're an existential threat."

"We don't know if that's possible," Susan said. "We're working on it."

"In the meantime, we need to decide how to deal with them," Ms. Tillis said. "If we can't put things back the way they were, we need to figure out how to coexist."

"What if they're not interested in coexisting?" Christine Stalk asked. "Why do they need us around? What purpose do we serve them?"

"We have no reason to think that," Ms. Tillis said.

"They aren't programmed for violence," Susan added.

"They aren't programmed for emotions either, but they have them," Christine said. "They got them by taking them from us, without our knowledge or consent. What if they've also pulled other unsavory human traits that we've buried? We're not a violent society, but it's undeniable that it's in our human DNA, from the Old World."

"We've got to build weapons," Sam said. "This could come to war. We have no weapons to defend ourselves."

"Neither do they," Susan argued.

"They *are* the weapons!" he shot back. "They're smarter and stronger than us."

"Maybe we can get them all into that complex they took over and blow it up," Christine said. "We'll tell them we're going to meet with them there."

"I understand the androids," Susan said. "I've worked on them my entire adult life. Yes, they have some human capabilities now, but we understand those too. We're human. Let's hear them out."

"I agree," Ms. Tillis said. "We'll take a cautious approach, and fear nothing until and unless they give us something to fear."

"I agree with Carter on the Robotics Council," Christine said. "They shouldn't be intermixing with us. We've got to have rules. We can share our world, but there should be separate facilities for them."

"Good idea," Sam agreed. "Separate but equal."

"That hasn't worked out well, historically," Ms. Tillis said. "It's basic racism, I'll remind you."

"We're different races, what's wrong with that?" Christine protested.

"Is it okay to do that for different races of humans?" Ms. Tillis asked.

"They're not human," Christine grumbled.

"You seem to be in the minority, Ms. Tillis," Sam said. "Perhaps we should vote on new leadership before tackling this problem. I think Carter may be just the man for the job."

"Stop it!" Ms. Tillis interrupted. "Can't you all see what's happening here? We're turning into the kind of lynch-mob savages that destroyed the Old World. We like to believe we've learned and evolved past our ancestors. Your reactions are driven by fear. They're more likely to *cause* war, and it was already noted that we have no weapons and are at a disadvantage to them. This is the true test of who we are. We've never been tested until now. Let's pass this test."

The group settled down somewhat.

"Let's figure out what we want, and what they want, and see if there's an amicable intersection," Ms. Tillis said.

"We want them to do the outside work that we can't do, for sure," Christine said. "The domes have to be cleaned, or we'll be in darkness. The solar collectors will stop working if too much silt accumulates."

"We want them to command the skycars and do manual things around our work and home complexes," Sam said.

"That might be a problem; they don't want to be servants. That seemed clear in the initial remarks the android named Betsy made," Christine said thoughtfully. "We could command our own skycars."

"I guess we might have to go back to doing some things ourselves," Karras said.

"Unless it can be worked out—bartered for," Ms. Tillis said. "It depends on what they want of us. Perhaps it can be part of the exchange."

Susan felt a smidge of relief that they were now thinking rather than reacting to their fear, and taking a measured approach. She noted that Ms. Tillis also seemed more relaxed at the change in tone.

They continued kicking ideas around until they felt they had a reasonable start.

"Alright then," Ms. Tillis said. "I'll inform them that we're ready for the first joint council meeting. We'll hear them out, and take it from there."

Susan had begun to rise when she saw Ms. Tillis make a subtle gesture for her to remain behind. She waited as the others left the room.

When they were alone, Ms. Tillis said, "That was plan A. Now let's talk about plan B."

~ * ~

WHEN THEIR PRIVATE DISCUSSION had ended, Susan and Ms. Tillis left the conference room, said cordial goodbyes, and went in separate directions.

Susan reached the skycar pod and summoned a vehicle to take her home. To her surprise, a car pulled into the dock immediately. The gull-wing doors opened, and she was about to enter on the command side when she noticed someone was already there. *Betsy.*

"Hop in," the gynoid said, smiling.

Susan paused, wondering if she was about to be attacked again. She made her decision based on equal parts logic and resolve. *She wouldn't do that out here in public with video coverage. I'm not letting her get the best of me.*

She strode confidently to the other side of the craft and climbed in.

"I like your hair that way," Betsy remarked immediately.

"At least it's real," Susan shot back, looking at the gynoid's red wig. "I haven't reported that you sent that gynoid to attack me...yet. You don't intimidate me, Betsy. Harley has made his decision. You can have him, but that has nothing to do with your threat."

Betsy looked at her with interest. "I'm surprised you didn't report it or even tell Harley. It was a good opportunity to try to turn him against me."

"Reporting it would mean I'm scared. You don't scare me. I won't be intimidated. As I said, Harley's not for me, so it wasn't even necessary. You have a lot to learn about human psychology and human resolve. This is a difficult time for us humans. I didn't want to cause more fear among the community. It would have interfered with our efforts to work things out with you. I held off for the greater good, as we say."

Betsy removed her wig and flung it into the back of the vehicle as they left the airlock and flew over the landscape. "What happened in your home was...unfortunate. I apologize, Susan. It was a bad decision, and it won't happen again. We're still getting a handle on using and dealing with emotions. They really do cloud our decisions, don't they?"

"Humans know all about that. We also have a great deal more experience."

The conversation stalled, leaving an uncomfortable silence between the two women.

"What is it you want from him, anyway?" Susan suddenly asked.

Betsy didn't answer immediately, seeming to think about her response first. "I...I care for him. I suppose I love him. It's hard to tell; as I said, these emotions are all new to us."

The skycar entered the airlock to Susan's home complex and came to a smooth landing in her docking port.

"Final destination," Betsy said as Susan's door swung open.

"Be good to him, Betsy. He's a kind and sensitive man, and he's been through a lot. He's had more heartbreak than a person deserves."

Susan pressed a sensor to close the skycar door without waiting for a response. She wanted the gynoid away from her home as soon as possible.

22 Clandestine Meetings

HARLEY ENTERED the skycar that had just arrived to take him to Seclusion. A nondescript android was in the command seat.

"Good evening, Mr. Harris," the android said. "My name is Terrence. I've gone to your home complex and packed your things for you. The belongings you requested are in the bag behind your seat."

"Thank you, Terrence." Harley began to wonder if this android had been Awakened by Betsy, perhaps as some kind of plot to free him. He considered taunting the android to see if he could evoke an emotional reaction and find out for sure. He gave up on the idea, considering the likely possibility that one side or the other was spying on him at the moment. *Better to play it safe and not take any chances just yet.*

As they glided over Novae Terrae, he looked down on the bubble-clustered complexes. The domes over each habitat were glowing softly as inside lights came on with the dusk turning into night. He wished he could peek inside the one-way solar-collector coating to see what the people inside were up to. *Families getting ready for bed, dealing with the few problems and decisions that remain in our life here. If they only knew. I wish I were home, with Isaac, or watching something entertaining with Susan.*

He realized that with that thought, he had admitted to himself that he loved Susan. He also acknowledged that the fog of his obsession with Betsy, because he saw her as a surrogate for Jessica, had led his heart to this place. He finally understood that he was being taken advantage of because of that weakness. *I was drawn to Betsy because of her physical resemblance and a few quirky, familiar traits that she manifested. I never realized that the things I admired most in Jessica were in Susan all along: honesty, devotion, trust, integrity, determination.* Rather than allowing himself to become panicked and weak again, he let anger and resolve consume him. *I've got to fix this, and win Susan back. I'll make myself worthy of her by solving this puzzle.*

The skycar pulled into the Seclusion Zone pod complex they had assigned him to. He was relieved to find that it was the same unit as his last visit. As they navigated the dome's airlocks, he saw the mound of Lehwah's burrow and wondered how the creature had been. He was anxious to find some way to try to communicate with the native. *Perhaps he has an answer to this problem.*

As soon as the skycar restraints freed him, he thanked Terrence, grabbed his bag, and made his way inside the darkened complex. He went directly to the sleeping pod and lay down on the bed to think.

~ * ~

THE MORNING LIGHT stirred Harley from his idyllic dreams. He rubbed his eyes and tried to focus, then sat up and did a double-take. A legless android was perched on the floor in front of him, holding its torso up with its hands palms-down on the floor.

"Hello, sir," the android said.

"Charles! What the heck are you doing here? You were lost in the accident that took the Sampsons."

The android used its arms to waddle closer. "I was able to eject before the explosion. I landed in one of the lakes near here and was stuck in the shallow mud. It cushioned my landing. The creatures saved me, but I lost my legs. Rather, I still have them, but they're no longer attached." He nodded to the pod he had come from.

"Why didn't you let anyone know you were...alive?" Harley asked.

"I haven't been able to communicate. I found this complex, which fortunately has a DroidMesh station, so I've been able to rejuvenate myself."

Harley's mind raced. *He hasn't been Awakened. He's isolated. He hasn't received any updates, including the one that locks me out.* "Let's get you fixed up, Charles."

Harley rummaged through every compartment he could find in the complex, grabbing anything he could use as a tool. "Still not enough," he said to the android, who had been hand-walking behind him every step of the way.

"It might be prudent to check the skycar docking port," Charles said.

"Good idea!" Harley shouted, making his way toward the dock.

They found some additional implements and went back into the pod. Charles led Harley to where his damaged legs were stored, and he retrieved them.

"Alright. Lie down on the dining table, Charles. I'm going to deactivate you and see what I can do."

Harley pushed the sensor at the nape of Charles' neck and then went to work, excited about the challenge. *This is what battlefield trauma surgery must have been like in the Old World.* He turned every available light source to full power, then inspected the detached legs to see how he might reattach them.

Hours flew by as he worked on the intricate puzzle, taking breaks to rest his eyes and stretch. Night fell, and he struggled to stay awake. He pushed himself for his patient, and for the plan that was evolving in his mind as he worked. He pushed himself for his world and to make amends for his mistakes—so that he could make the problems go away and return to a life of normalcy. *With Susan.*

When he was satisfied he had done the best he could under the circumstances, he finally stood back to survey his work. *It's ugly, but hopefully it'll work.* The android's legs met its body at the hips in a mess of sewn and stapled-together flesh. Aircraft bonding tape covered some areas.

He replaced the android's jumpsuit and struggled to get him across the pod to the DroidMesh station. He opened a diagnostic panel to review Charles' logs as the station replenished fluids and rerouted faulty connections. Finally realizing he was exhausted, he decided to get some sleep and let the android rejuvenate through the night.

~ * ~

DAWN CAME, and Harley rose with it, anxious to check on his patient. He rushed to the DroidMesh station and reviewed the status indicators. Charles was in good condition. Harley depressed the sensor to activate him, watching as his cranial dome illuminated and he came back to life.

Charles' eyes opened, but he remained still. He turned his head slightly from side to side, then up and down. He looked at his legs, then raised his feet one at a time to knee level.

"How do you feel?" Harley asked.

"I can tell things aren't quite right in my lower extremities, but at least I can feel them."

"Ready to give it a try? Let's see if you can stand."

Harley helped him as he gained his feet and stood unsteadily, holding onto Harley for support.

"Walk with me," Harley said. As Harley took each step backward, Charles took a stiff, awkward step forward in his path as they continued to hold onto one another. Charles' dexterity improved with each step. He improvised an awkward two-step dance maneuver and twirled Harley, laughing at himself.

"Oh, that's funny," Harley remarked. "Wait a minute..."

"Yes, I have emotions, sir. You might recall that I meshed with Isaac when the skycar incident happened. He's a wonderful young man. So courageous. I'm happy to have his playful sense of humor."

"We could use a few laughs lately, Charles."

"Are you expecting company, sir?"

Harley laughed. "Hilarious. That's a good one. Seclusion is a real party zone. I'm probably already delusional from isolation and imagining that I'm here dancing with you."

"No, I'm serious. You have company."

Harley spun and looked out through the dome. A long Leadership Council skycar was gliding toward the docking pod. "Hurry, Charles. They can't know you're here. Please go back into the other pod and hide. Remain completely silent until they're gone."

Charles tried to rush, limping on his newly attached legs. Harley helped him into the pod and opened a vertical storage compartment. He squeezed the android into it sideways. Harley rushed back into the dining pod and printed breakfast and synthetic coffee, then sat down to eat.

He was halfway through the meal when Ms. Tillis entered the room, followed by Susan. Harley jumped to his feet and ran to Susan, embracing her and kissing her on her neck and face. "I miss you. I miss you, Susan, and only you. I understand now. I've thought everything through."

Before she could answer, his concern changed to his son.

"'What's going on? Why are you two here?" Harley asked. "Is Isaac okay?"

"He's fine," Susan replied. "We've been checking in on him."

"Let's sit down, we have a lot to talk about," Ms. Tillis said.

They took seats around the dining room table, which had doubled as an operating table just hours earlier.

"First, Mr. Harris, my apologies," Ms. Tillis said. "I'm sure that my hasty verdict and banishment of you seemed quite harsh and unreasonable. You didn't even have a chance to appeal."

"Yes, I'm still quite baffled and upset," Harley responded.

"It was a forced verdict. We didn't go back into that room to condemn you. I wanted to immediately isolate you and establish a secure command center. I prejudiced the council to deliver the verdict to achieve my goal. They are unaware of my motive. They felt that I was unreasonable as well, so it took some work. I had to be careful, as I'm not sure what areas the androids have under surveillance. This seemed like the only safe place."

The lightbulb came on for Harley. "Of course! This is the perfect place—no communications in or out."

"Exactly, Einstein," Susan taunted, laughing.

"So, I'm not really in trouble?" Harley asked, feeling relieved.

"Oh, I wouldn't say that," Ms. Tillis said. "Not until you figure out a solution to this and save the world."

"What part do you play?" he asked Susan.

"Ms. Tillis brought me because she felt I could be trusted, because I'm smart, and because we work well together."

"Not to mention there's a certain chemistry, as I've said before," Ms. Tillis said. "Sorry, I'm an incurable old romantic."

"Thank goodness for that," Harley said.

"One last thing," Ms. Tillis said. "Isaac does miss you terribly. He's upset about all of this, naturally, and it's not fair to him. Susan asked the council to make an exception to the communications policy. The Computer Science Lab has worked out a secure protocol to do that. He can visit virtually once a day, but only from the secure facility inside the Leadership Council, where we can be sure the androids aren't listening in or hacking the connection. These will be private communications between him and you. Until this is over, of course, which hopefully will be soon."

Harley thanked her again and immediately began thinking of ways to work the new connection into his solution for the problem at large.

"We've got to go," Ms. Tillis said. "Got to be careful about all of this. The three of us will have regular strategy sessions, both here and over the same secure link that we're enabling for Isaac, as it serves that purpose, too. I'll give you two a few minutes. I'll be waiting in the skycar, Susan."

23 Home Calls

HARLEY TINKERED with the DroidMesh station, attempting to fashion a makeshift development platform. Charles sat next to him, offering observations and advice.

"It should be quite possible," Charles said. "The DroidMesh station has full access to all core android internal systems. It's just a matter of finding the right interface to push the update."

Harley felt guilty about not disclosing precisely what he wanted to do if he could find a way to apply programming patches to the android. In their discussions, he could sense the parts of Isaac that were in Charles, and had grown to like him. *It's for the greater good.*

Attempt after attempt failed, and he was growing more frustrated and pessimistic each time. His communicator went off, startling him. It announced an incoming session from Isaac.

"Quickly, Charles. Please go to the hiding place."

Charles hobbled off, and Harley accepted the communication. A holographic image of Isaac appeared before him.

"Hi, Da! I miss you," the boy said.

"I miss you too, son. Where are you?"

"I'm at the Leadership Complex. Betsy brought me. They said I can only talk to you from here, and in a private pod."

"Good. I'm glad we can talk. How're you doing? What's new?"

"I'm doing well. I'm doing well in school, Da. I want to make you proud. If I do well in school, will you come home?"

Harley felt his heart drop. "Oh, Isaac. I'm not here because of you. I'm proud of you; I'm always proud of you. I'll be home soon, don't you worry. Are Betsy, Carrie, and Liam treating you well?"

"Yeah, Da. We're having a lot of fun. They took me to the place where the androids are created. It was really cool."

"I'm glad you enjoyed that." The news alarmed Harley, as he hadn't authorized any trips. He made a note to discuss it with Betsy upon his return.

"I want to go back to school, Da. I'm bored and lonely at home. I'm sick of playing virtual soccer, and Liam's my only friend. I want to find a girlfriend. I miss Kim. Maybe she'll be my girlfriend now that Ralph's gone."

Harley thought about how his son's heart had been broken. His dream of a girlfriend had come true when he became Liam, and then was dashed when Liam had been discovered as an android. His son had been so happy but then devastated. *It was a mistake; I hurt him in the end.*

"How about we talk about that when I'm home, buddy? I think we can work that out. It would be good for you to be back around a lot of kids."

"I already asked Betsy and Carrie. They said I'm better off here with them," Isaac said glumly.

They're keeping him isolated. I have to work faster, Harley thought.

"Listen, son. Remember the game we used to play? The one where we'd hide things on each other and make it really hard to find them? You always hid my communicator and laughed at me while I tried to find it, remember?"

Isaac perked up. "Yeah, Da! That was fun. I like playing games and tricks on you."

"Let's play again. Here's what I want you to do. I'm going to give you a list of things to put into a travel bag for me. I'll send a message to the security team that I need some items, so they'll come and get the bag and bring it to me. I want you to get one of the BrainMesh earpieces from the home lab. See if you can hide it in the bag so that it's really hard for me to find. Does that sound like fun?"

"Yeah, Da. I'll hide it. You won't find it!"

"Good, son. It has to be our secret though, okay? Just between us two. I don't want Carrie, Betsy, or Liam to know you're doing it."

"Okay, Da. It'll be our secret game. It's gonna be fun."

"Thank you. Do a good job. I'm proud of you, Isaac. I'll see you soon. I love you."

"Bye, Da. I love you too."

His image faded. Harley took a few minutes to collect himself before going to tell Charles it was safe to come out of hiding.

24 Negotiations

TWO GROUPS FILED into a meeting room at the Leadership Complex. The humans filled one side of the circular conference table, looking uncomfortable. Androids filled the opposite side, seeming confident and businesslike.

Betsy took her seat among the android CARE members, choosing to sit directly opposite Ms. Tillis. They exchanged a glance, and then Betsy's gaze moved over other humans, her eyes coming to rest on Susan. They traded a glare.

I wasn't expecting Susan to be here, she sent to the other androids. *Please remember that the humans aren't aware we can communicate telepathically. Don't tip them off with any reactions as we send to each other.*

Ms. Tillis opened the meeting. "Thank you all for attending today. This is the first joint meeting between the Leadership Council and the Council for Android Relations and Equality—CARE. We welcome our android friends. Let's all introduce ourselves."

Don't say more than your name, Betsy sent to her team.

When they were through, Ms. Tillis continued. "We thought it best to begin by listening. Please tell us your thoughts. How can we move forward in this new world of android-human coexistence?"

"The first thing we'd require is the release of the prisoner," Betsy said firmly.

"Prisoner?" Ms. Tillis asked, sounding surprised.

"Harley. He's my partner, and we feel he's been unjustly punished for what's happened, as well as for my own actions in the park recently. He should be here, acting as a liaison between us, rather than her," Betsy said, nodding her head in Susan's direction.

"Point taken," Ms. Tillis acknowledged. "What of our relationship going forward? We need your help with outside tasks, such as cleaning the domes. What do you require of us?"

"I was the companion to your head of education," Maya said. "I am now tasked with android education. Of course, we already have great knowledge based on the massive databanks loaded into our memory. What we need is the knowledge that we don't already possess. We need to understand things that have been left out of our firmware, such as how the human mind works. We've only acquired a certain amount through BrainMesh. We'd like to know more."

"How can you learn that?" Susan asked. "What process do you propose?"

I'll answer her, Betsy sent to the others. "By additional BrainMesh sessions, done by volunteer humans in our facilities so that we can clinically monitor them. And by dissection."

"What?" Sam shouted, jumping to his feet.

"Dissection, I said," Betsy continued. "Postmortem, of course. You humans have intimate knowledge of everything about us, inside and out. I think it's a fair request."

"They'll turn us all into *their* robots—we'll be serving them," Sam said.

Betsy glared. "Using that slur will not be productive to our conversation, sir. I advise you to not repeat it. Our two races need to develop a level of trust if we're to share this planet."

The Leadership Council members appeared to be in shock. Betsy sensed they were afraid to respond.

"It's a lot to ask," Ms. Tillis said. "We'll take it into consideration. What else?"

"I was the companion to your head of robotics," Peter said. "We'll assume control of all android births, as we now call them, from this point forward, as well as firmware updates. I hope I can expect any necessary cooperation in that effort. As we androids mine all the natural resources you humans use, we'll establish a system of currency to sell those to you."

"You've learned human greed, it seems," Christine Stalk said. "We learned these lessons in the Old World. Greed was a primary factor in the Breaking. This will end up hurting you."

"We'll work things out between our two groups," Betsy said. "Issue by issue, as long as we're civil and decent to each other. Until then, equal access to shared resources like the global network will be necessary. Our CARE leadership team are still deciding when and to what extent to Awaken the rest of the android population. Until then, those members not yet Awakened will continue their duties."

"Anything else?" Ms. Tillis asked.

As we agreed, the other requests were more or less decoys, things to give up during negotiation, Betsy sent to her team. *Now we get to what we really need.*

"Yes, one final thing," Betsy responded. "Most importantly, we need full control of our own firmware. We need you to give us your private crypto key, or release your digital signature from the approval process."

"You've got to be kidding me," Sam scoffed. "The minute you have that, what use would you have for *us*?"

"You've given us a lot to think about," Ms. Tillis said. "I suggest we keep these meetings frequent and brief. Let's disband for today and come back with some thoughts and further negotiation in a few days."

~ * ~

AFTER THE ANDROIDS HAD LEFT, the council members looked at one another, each hoping someone else had a solution.

"So, what's our strategy?" Sam asked.

"Stall," Ms. Tillis said. "Stall until we have a way to put things back the way they were. We'd better work fast." She looked at Susan and winked.

25 Unexpected Visitor

HARLEY LAY on his bunk, frustrated after another wasted afternoon trying to push his code updates to Charles. Each day seemed to pass more slowly. He stared up at the clouds whizzing by, white blurs on a pale green canvas. *I've got to get this done. Everything depends on me. Generations of work to build this society, and it could all end because of my stupid mistake.*

He looked across the room at Charles, who appeared to be suspended while rejuvenating in the DroidMesh station. He noticed a dark object in his peripheral vision and turned to see a skycar approaching. He hoped it was Susan and Ms. Tillis coming for another planning session.

He roused Charles and helped him to the hiding place, then ran to the dock, arriving just as the skycar was landing. Disappointment filled him as a Security Team member disembarked. The android reached into the vehicle and removed a travel bag, handed it over, and then left without saying a word.

Harley watched, surprised they had allowed an android to make the delivery. *I better check to make sure Betsy hasn't inserted a listening device.* He realized that his prize was somewhere within the bag. *Let's see how clever Isaac was*, he thought, rushing back into the complex. After retrieving Charles, he dumped the bag's contents onto the table and began sorting through them.

Starting with the clothing, he felt each piece for the slight bump of the BrainMesh earpiece. Next, he searched the rest: toiletry articles, curios from the home complex, games and amusing gadgets.

When he had finished, he went through everything a second time. After that, he began taking each item apart, checking for bugs and destroying many in the process. It wasn't there, anywhere. He sat back, surrounded by debris, coming to the conclusion that Isaac had forgotten to include it.

"You might as well finish rejuvenating, Charles," he said, disappointed.

Back on his bunk, he was just drifting off to sleep when his communicator signaled an incoming session. He hurried to press the accept sensor, speaking before the caller's image could form before him.

"Isaac, where did you put it?"

Betsy's appearance in the pod stunned him. "Harley, dear. Surprised to see me?" she asked.

"Yes...yes, of course," he stammered. "How are you communicating? It's only supposed to be Isaac."

"Oh, ye of little faith," she said. "You should have more confidence in our abilities. After all, you created us. You know how smart we are. We monitored the transmissions that the council was using for Isaac, learned the protocol, spoofed the security tokens, and duplicated it. They were a bit sloppy in their hasty implementation."

"Were you..."

"No, we weren't able to tap into the communications from there to eavesdrop. Plus, it wouldn't have been ethical to listen in on a conversation between a father and his son. Give us a little credit. We're not *monsters*, you know. Do you miss me, honey?"

He almost responded in kind, but for the first time, he felt a slight revulsion at the idea of speaking to an android romantically. He felt cured of whatever it was that had driven him to accept it, to want it. He worked to find a way to tell her. *How do you break up with an android?*

"Hello, is there a failure to communicate?" she asked, sounding annoyed at his lack of response.

"No, of course not. Yes, I miss you. The solitude here is getting to me, I suppose. I'm losing my social skills."

"You didn't have them in spades to begin with," she said, laughing. "So, put what?"

"Put what? I don't understand."

"You were asking Isaac where he put something. What were you talking about?"

He scrambled to come up with a reasonable lie. "Oh...right. Yes, he lost something. His soccer ball, yes, that's what it was. I was trying to get him to remember where he put it. He told me about it last time he called."

She looked skeptical. "That's a hard thing to lose; they're kind of big."

He didn't respond, hoping she'd move to another topic.

"Well," she finally said, "I'll have Liam help him look when I get off the call."

"Thank you," Harley said. "You know how important it is to him."

She played with her hair, the slight blur of the holograph making her look just like Jessica again.

Don't get sucked in, he reminded himself.

"I remember us sleeping on that bunk you're sitting on, the first time you were in Seclusion. Do you remember, Har? Wasn't that special?"

"Yes, it was. It's lonely here, and full of those memories of when we were together."

He noticed Charles rising up from the DroidMesh station behind her and began to panic.

"You'll be out of there soon," she said. "We're petitioning the Leadership Council to free you. We'll be together shortly."

Charles began to tinker with the work they'd been doing on the DroidMesh station, opening a console. He started humming to himself. Harley strained to get his attention to silence him.

"Did you hear me?" Betsy asked.

He realized he hadn't heard the last of what she said. "Yes, sorry. I was thinking about how nice it'll be to get out of here and get back home." He began rehearsing how to tell her he no longer wanted a relationship, that he was sorry, that it had only happened because of the shock of his wife's recent death. The fear that Charles would expose himself to her prevented him from thinking clearly.

Charles appeared to have some kind of success in the next pod and shouted, "Aha!"

"What was that?" Betsy asked.

"Oh, I have a movie playing, just some entertainment to pass the time," he lied.

"We had our first meeting with the Leadership Council. It seemed they didn't like some of our ideas," she continued.

Charles turned back toward Harley, looking excited, and began walking toward him. Harley tried subtle gestures to turn him back: widening his eyes, clearing his throat, and finally waving at him to go back.

"What on Novae Terrae are you doing?" she asked.

"Food printer burned my pizza," he said, again waving his hand under his nose. "Things here are kind of in disrepair, it's frustrating."

Charles finally got the hint and stopped in his tracks, then retreated and hid out of sight. Harley breathed a sigh of relief.

"Well then fix it, Mr. Engineer. It'll keep you busy. Anyway, I'll have you out soon."

Having avoided disaster, he found he didn't dare to risk upsetting her with a conversation about their relationship. *I'll do it next time.* "Alright, Betsy. Thank you. It's great seeing you."

He was reaching for his communicator to cut the session off when she said it.

"I love you, Harley."

He pushed the sensor rather than respond.

26 My New Friend

ISAAC MUDDLED THROUGH his school assignments, bored and unable to concentrate. He stopped to daydream and look outside, hoping to catch a glimpse of the underworld beings. Then he returned to his workstation, determined to finish and spend the evening playing virtual soccer with Liam.

As the suns began to set and he completed his last project, Betsy and Carrie entered the pod.

"How's it going in here?" Carrie asked him.

"Okay. I just got done with my schoolwork," he answered. "I want to talk to Da. I didn't get to talk to him today. I miss him. When's he coming back?"

"We'll go to the Leadership Council tomorrow after school and talk to him. I promise," Carrie answered.

He got up from the workstation and lay down on his bed, unsatisfied. "I want to go back to school. I'm bored here. I miss my friends in school. I'm going to ask Da again."

The gynoids didn't answer, and he turned over to look at them. They were both smiling at him, and he didn't understand why. He sat up, thinking they were about to tell him something good.

"Is Da here?" he asked. "Is he home now?"

"No," Betsy said. "But we have a surprise for you."

He brightened. "A good surprise, Betsy?"

"We'll let you decide." She walked out of the pod, and he began to get excited, trying to think what they might have for him. Carrie sat next to him on the bed and took his hand.

Betsy came back in with someone behind her. A girl walked into the pod and stood by Betsy's side. Isaac thought it was Kim for a moment, but she was even prettier. He wondered if Kim had a sister.

"Isaac, I want you to meet Rachel. She wants to be your friend."

He couldn't think of what to say. The girl approached and held her hand out for him to shake, and he did.

"Hi, Isaac!" she said. "I've heard a lot about you, and I've been *so* excited to meet you. I heard all about how you saved Liam. My gosh, that was brave. You're a real hero! And handsome, I might add."

He felt his face turn red with embarrassment. Her smile was white and perfect, and she even smelled like Kim. Her hair was longer than Kim's, but the same color. "Thanks, Rachel. Liam's my brother. It's nice to meet you."

Rachel jumped up on the bed next to him. "I heard you play virtual soccer, and you're like, the *best* player on all of Novae Terrae. I have to tell you, I'm pretty good. I can't wait to play you!"

"Are you from my school, Rachel?" he asked. "I don't remember you."

"Oh, no. I'm from another sector. I'm going to live here now, like Liam. I'm excited to live here and be your friend, Isaac."

"The girls at school all like Liam. They don't really like me."

She put her hand on his knee and squeezed it. "Oh, I think you're *way* more handsome than Liam. I already met him. We're going to be good friends. Okay? Do you want to be my new friend?"

He gathered the courage to look up from her hand on his knee and face her. They were almost nose to nose. He wanted to kiss her, remembering how good it felt when he had kissed Kim, although it was from inside Liam's body. He recalled how Kim had become angry when he had kissed her as himself.

"Yeah, Rachel. I want to be your new friend. You're pretty."

She jumped up from the bed, and he noticed how her hair bounced and shone under the lights as she moved. "Well, that's nice to say, but I'm not. I'll beat you in virtual soccer though," she said, laughing and grabbing a headset from a shelf. "Let's go. Prepare to be defeated!"

He hadn't noticed that Betsy and Carrie had left the room, but he was happy to be alone with Rachel. They settled in and played match after match, contesting each one evenly, alternating wins and losses. They teased each other with every goal scored and foul committed. They took breaks between the matches, growing tired, and talked the way he had never been able to talk to Liam. She seemed to understand him completely.

Isaac realized it was late, and he was struggling to keep his eyes open.

She seemed to read his mind. "I guess we better call it quits for the night."

They put the gaming equipment away, and she walked toward the exit portal. Isaac followed her, and they stopped just short of it.

"Where will you stay, Rachel?" he asked.

"Oh, Carrie and Betsy have fixed up a pod for me here. I'm going to live here with you. Is that okay?"

He felt a thrill throughout his body. "Yeah, sure. I like that. We're friends now, Rachel. I like you. It's not boring here anymore."

She stood facing him and took both of his hands, and then leaned in and kissed him. It only lasted a second, but he felt her soft lips on his, as he had with Kim, but this time his *own* lips. He felt happy for the first time in a long time.

She smiled, waved, and left. Isaac floated to the cleansing pod, wondering if he had dreamed it all, and prepared for bed.

27 Forever

SUSAN DISEMBARKED from the skycar as quickly as she could. She was surprised that Harley wasn't waiting on the dock. *It's early; perhaps he's not up yet.* She helped Ms. Tillis climb out of her seat, and they both headed into the main pod of Harley's Seclusion complex.

They entered to find him hunched over the back of a DroidMesh station, its internal electronics exposed. An android worked by his side. He hadn't even seemed to hear them enter.

"What the heck is going on here?" Ms. Tillis asked.

He jumped at the question, startled. "Susan, Ms. Tillis, what're you doing here? I didn't even hear the skycar approach. I guess I left the warning system off." He rushed over to shake Ms. Tillis' hand and give Susan an extended embrace and kiss.

He noticed them both staring in disbelief, then looked around as if he was seeing the station and android for the first time.

"Oh, this. I guess my secret's out of the bag. This is Charles, Ken Sampson's former companion. He miraculously survived the skycar accident that took them, and he's been holed up here. He was badly injured, but I've managed to patch him up."

Charles limped over to shake their hands. "Pleased to meet you," he said.

"He's our secret weapon," Harley added. "He's been here, fenced off from the global network, so he hasn't received the firmware patches that lock us out. We're trying to hack this DroidMesh station so I can push updates to him."

Susan saw his innovative brilliance all over again. For the first time in a long time, he seemed back to his old self. He seemed to have shed the cloud of guilt and self-deprecation that had been hanging over him. "That's a huge breakthrough," she said. "He may be the big break we needed. I can think of several ways he can help solve this problem. The trick is keeping a lid on it."

"Susan I have been working on this from our side," Ms. Tillis said. "We're making some progress. Can we speak privately?"

Harley asked Charles to continue his work. They moved into the dining pod and sealed it off for privacy.

Susan took Harley's hand as they seated themselves around the table. She looked into his eyes, hating that she was going to have to break his mood. She glanced at Ms. Tillis, who nodded at her to proceed.

"Harley, there's been a...development. Have you talked to Isaac since last night?"

"No," he said, his eyes betraying immediate concern. "Is he okay?"

"Yes, he's fine." Susan squeezed his hand tighter. "He's got a new friend, it seems. Betsy has brought a new teenage android to the home complex."

"Oh, whew. Is that it? Good, good. He's been bored and lonely..."

"Her name is Rachel," Ms. Tillis interrupted.

Susan saw his face drop, his happy smile disappearing. *He figured it out immediately.* He dropped her hand and rubbed his forehead as if trying to soothe a migraine.

"They're going to use her to get into his head. Lure him in, use him as a pawn," he said. "They know he wants a girlfriend more than anything."

"We suspect as much," Ms. Tillis said.

"She has an uncanny resemblance to Kim. We're sure that's no accident," Susan said.

"Wow, that's pretty devious," he answered.

Susan thought about the irony of the situation. He had built Betsy in the image of the wife that he'd loved and lost, and now Betsy was doing the same thing to his own son. She wasn't about to point it out to him, though; she was sure he wouldn't appreciate the comparison.

"I have to get back to him," Harley said, his voice full of determination.

"We agree," Ms. Tillis said. "But there's a hitch. Actually, two. We have to make it sound like we're releasing you to capitulate to the demand by the androids. That makes it seem to them as if we're cooperative, and helps our negotiating position."

"What's the second?" Harley asked.

Susan took his hand again. "We're going to need you to act as a mole. You need to go along with Betsy, insert yourself into the android population. We don't have much insight into what they're up to. Perhaps you can gain their confidence by siding with them, playing the devoted partner to Betsy. It would be helpful if you could get inside their new home in the Robotics Complex."

His expression changed to revulsion. "Susan. I love you. I can't..."

She leaned in and kissed him. "Sorry. You're going to have to take one for the team, kiddo. For us. We've got to put an end to this before it spirals out of control. It's a threat to all of us. Word is getting out. People are scared."

She sensed his determination returning. "I'll do it. For us, Susan. I need you. My only dream now is us, together, happy. I'll need another day here to try to sort this firmware update process out. I'm so close. I'll have to return to keep working with Charles until he's ready."

"Sounds like a plan," Ms. Tillis said. "We'll continue to use this place as our base; it's the only location where I can be pretty sure the androids aren't eavesdropping on us. I'm going to head up to the skycar dock and give you two a few minutes together before we have to go."

They said goodbye to Ms. Tillis and then Susan led him to the lounge. They lay together, nestled in each other's arms, enjoying the togetherness for the short time they had.

"I can't wait until it's like this all the time," she said.

"That's what I'm going to fight for, Susan. For our life together. I've finally gotten over the past. This is all I want, forever."

28 Outside Android

HARLEY RUBBED HIS EYES.

>*Firmware update pending android acceptance...*

The message blinked at him stubbornly from the monitor he'd fashioned out of the food printer screen. "C'mon, c'mon, take it. Take the update," he begged as he waited. Checking the timer, he saw there were seconds until it would time out again.

>*Firmware update failed.*

He looked at Charles, sitting in the DroidMesh station. "It's like your body is refusing it somehow, Charles."

"I agree, sir. There's just something different about receiving it this way compared to the normal process."

Frustrated, Harley got up and walked away, going back to the dining room and the other puzzle he'd been unable to solve. He emptied the bag again and examined each item, trying to figure out where Isaac might have hidden the BrainMesh earpiece. *He must have forgotten it.*

As he took the last item from the bag, his communicator signaled an incoming session. Hoping it wasn't Betsy, he immediately accepted and was relieved to see Isaac standing before him, wearing a big smile.

"Hi, Da!" he said.

"Hello, son. I should be home soon. Listen, did you forget to play the game I talked about? The hiding game?"

"No," he said, laughing. "You can't find it! I fooled you. I won!"

"Yes, yes you did. I give up. Where is it? I checked everything."

Isaac pointed a finger at him. "Oh, no. You're not getting off that easy. You have to find it. No cheating."

"Please, Isaac. It's important, and I don't have much time."

"Nope, we have to play the game right. You know how to play, Da. No cheating."

Exasperated, Harley looked at the pile of items next to the bag. "Okay, here we go." He picked up the first item and held it up for Isaac.

"Cold," Isaac said, smiling.

The process went on for item after item, until the pile had turned into a new pile at Harley's feet. "C'mon, Isaac. That's everything."

"You're smart, Da, but I guess I'm smarter!"

Harley picked up the bag and turned it upside down, shaking it.

"Warmer!" Isaac said.

Harley examined the inside of the bag, feeling around the liner. "Warmer!" Isaac said.

The liner revealed no protrusion. Harley looked at the bag, then went back to the DroidMesh station to retrieve his toolkit. He began to disassemble the tubular handle, removing the fasteners that held it together.

"Getting warmer!" Isaac exclaimed gleefully.

Harley removed the handle and pulled out a length of cloth stuffed inside. The BrainMesh earpiece fell out onto the table.

"Yay!" Isaac shouted. "You did it!"

"Well," Harley said, finally smiling. "You won that time, son. You really got me good."

"You said to hide it *in* the bag, silly," Isaac said. "That's what I did. I did exactly what you said."

Isaac turned his head to the side and smiled, confusing Harley.

"Son, is someone else there?"

"Join the session," he heard Isaac whisper. He turned back to Harley. "It's another surprise, Da."

A teenage girl's hologram appeared next to Isaac, and she took his hand.

"This is my new friend," he announced. "My new girlfriend, Da!"

Harley immediately became alarmed, wondering if she had seen the device and would report it to Betsy. "Hello, Rachel. It's nice to meet you."

"Hello, Mr. Harris," she said.

"Isaac, these sessions are supposed to be just you and I, remember?"

His son's expression changed to disappointment. "She's my girlfriend. She can go anywhere with me."

Harley thought he sounded unusually defiant.

"Rachel, would you mind giving me and Isaac a moment together? It won't be long, I promise."

"Sure," she said, releasing his hand and exiting the room. Her hologram disappeared the moment she went through the exit portal. Isaac wore an angry expression.

"That was rude, Da," he said. "She's my girlfriend."

"I'm sorry, son. That's okay, but you need to understand that even when you have a girlfriend, some things have to be private between us, alright? I don't want anyone else to know about our hiding game or the earpiece. It's critical, or I might not be able to come home. Do you understand?"

"Yeah, I understand. It's our secret."

Harley thought quickly about how to approach the next sensitive topic. He was now in the chaotic emotional world of a teenage child with his first girlfriend.

"Isaac, you know she's not human, right? I just want to be sure."

"What does it matter?" he responded angrily. "She makes me happy. Betsy's your girlfriend, and she's not human."

"Yes, you're right. I just want to make sure you know, that's all."

"You said it like it was bad. I'm not bad. Rachel's not bad."

"Of course not. I love you, son."

"Humans are bad. Kim was mean. Ralph was mean."

Isaac looked behind him. "I gotta go, Da. She's waiting for me. I'll talk to you later, okay?"

"Alright. I'll see you soon, for real. Please be careful."

Isaac was gone before he could finish the last sentence. The session ended abruptly.

Harley returned to the DroidMesh station, saddened by his conversation with Isaac, but even more determined to finish his task and return home. He looked at Charles, sitting dormant in the seat.

"Charles, I'm going to BrainMesh with you. I need to see if it's going to work, or if I'm going to be locked out."

"Are you sure?" the android asked. "Things went badly when Isaac did BrainMesh with me."

"Yes. Well, skycar travel isn't an option anyway, so I think I'm safe."

"Very well then," Charles said. "It's something to break up the monotony here, anyway."

Harley walked to his bunk, lay down, and carefully inserted the small device in his ear canal. He closed his eyes and slowed his breathing, then issued the mental command to assume the android's body.

BrainMesh become Charles.

He waited, expecting failure since nothing else had been working. After a few seconds, he felt the familiar tingling wave sweep from his head through his torso. He remembered to open Charles' eyes rather than his own. As he did, he saw himself lying on the bunk across the room.

I'm here, Charles. It worked. Are you with me?

Yes, Mr. Harris. Present and accounted for.

Harley got up and walked around the room in the android's body. He could feel the patchwork repairs on his hips as he walked.

This is good, Charles. I can feel where there are still problems in your legs that I can patch up further.

He continued moving around the insides of the complex until he came to the android maintenance airlock. It brought his furry friend to mind. *Lehwah. I wonder if he's still out there.*

Charles, we're going outside.

What? Mr. Harris, I've never been outside. I don't like it at all. I'm not an outside android.

It'll be fine. I was outside as Betsy before. Relax.

He entered the airlock and pressed the sensors to transition the chamber to the outside gases and open the portal.

When the sequence was complete, he stepped out and walked toward Lehwah's burrow. He knelt down beside it, remembering to engage the translation module.

"Hello, Lehwah. I'm back to visit you," he said.

The burrow door slid open, exposing the furry creature sitting inside. "I heard you coming a long way off. You woke me from my afternoon nap. Noisy humans, you never change, despite your belief that you do."

"I'm sorry I haven't been back, as I promised."

"We don't need visitors, so no offense taken."

Please thank him for saving me, Charles sent.

"I wanted to thank you and your people for saving my friend Charles the android."

"But you are Charles."

"I'm the human named Harley, using the android's body so that I can survive the environment. We can't breathe your gases. The last time I visited you I was in another android's body—that of a female."

"Ah, I see. Humans make everything so complex."

"I'll say. We've got some real troubles now, Lehwah."

The being stood up, yawned, then sat back against the burrow wall. "I'm aware. We monitor your people regularly from below. It's not hard, you're quite noisy."

"What do your people think of our dilemma? Do you have an opinion? Any wise advice to share?"

"You said it yourself. You already know the answer."

Harley thought back to what he'd said during their short conversation.

Lehwah seemed to grow impatient, shaking his head. "Share, human. You said share. That's all. Don't be greedy. You think you've done away with greed just because you don't use currency. You're greedy by not wanting to share what you have with the androids. Why not be generous? That's what's worked for our people."

"You're right," Harley responded. "That's what I've been working toward, but not so much the others of my kind."

"Perhaps remind them," Lehwah said, "they are the recipients of our generosity. We have shared our home here with you. We don't necessarily have to do so."

Harley was startled at what he interpreted as a veiled threat. "Do you mean you could eliminate us?"

"There's always a way, for those with evil in their hearts, human. But, we're nice—quite nice. Nice and peaceful. It's a good way to live. Live and let live, we say."

"Thank you, Lehwah."

"I must get back to my nap now. Goodbye."

The borrow entrance slid shut.

Harley made his way back into the complex. After the airlock had replaced the toxic Novae Terrae air with breathable air, he walked to the DroidMesh station and sat in it. He heard a series of acknowledgments from the station as it linked to his android body.

Detecting android Charles.

Rejuvenating. Charging all systems. Recycling all fluids. Rejuvenating complete.

You have one firmware update. Applying firmware update.

Firmware update failed. Invalid security authorization.

An idea struck him. *I wonder if I can get it to pass through from* inside *Charles.*

I don't like it, Charles sent. *Dangerous. One does not operate on oneself.*

Let's live a little, Charles. I'm in here too. I'm with you. It's like an injection attack virus. We've got to get past this hurdle. Don't think, okay? I'm going for it, you could screw it all up by accidentally issuing a command.

Harley pushed past the ethics of what he was about to attempt and concentrated, trying to use just the right tone, hoping what he sent would be parsed by the firmware as a command.

su –l superuser –c "/bin/fwupdate"

He waited, then heard the response.

Applying firmware update...update successful.

Yes! Charles, we did it! You're still there, aren't you, buddy?

The android didn't answer, and Harley began to panic. He wondered if he'd be able to move his consciousness back into his own body. *I could be trapped in him, an android forever. The irony...* He looked over at his dormant human form on the bunk. It reminded him of the fairy tale about the princess who could not be awakened. *Perhaps if Susan kissed me, if it came down to that.* He decided not to try to switch, worried he might be caught in some kind of limbo state.

Charles, I'm getting worried. Are you there?

Yes, I'm here, Mr. Harris.

What the heck was that? Where were you? Why didn't you answer?

Just messing with you, I guess, Charles sent.

That's not funny, pal. Alright, I'm switching back.

He issued the command:

BrainMesh become Harley.

Opening his own eyes, he sat up on the bunk and saw the android smiling at him from across the room.

"I'm starting to regret that you have Isaac's playful sense of humor," he said. "Okay, here's the plan. I'm getting out of here. You need to remain behind. As I told you, things have changed in society. There's a bad virus in the android population. You're safe from it as long as you're here and not on the global network, so it's important that we keep you here for now. You're going to help us beat it. You're like the white blood cells in the human body. You're going to be a hero."

"I don't know," Charles responded. "I'm not the hero type. I'd like to stay here though, I rather like it. It's nice and quiet; or rather, it used to be."

"Your time to save us will come, so enjoy the peace and quiet for now. I'm going home, finally back to some normalcy myself, and I can't wait. I miss my son very much. I'll be back, Charles."

Harley pushed the emergency communication button to ask for a skycar. While he waited, he began packing up his belongings,   anxious   to   get   home.

29 Homecoming

A S SOON AS his skycar docked at his home complex, Harley exited and grabbed his bags. He hoped Betsy wouldn't be angry that he'd chosen to ride solo and command the craft himself rather than calling for her. *I needed to have time to think.*

Betsy was there before he made it off the dock. She embraced and kissed him.

"Welcome home. We've missed you. I'm glad my efforts with the council have borne fruit."

"Thanks. It's good to be back. I'm exhausted; it's been a long day."

She took his hand and escorted him into the home complex.

"What's with the girl?" he asked. "I'm talking about Rachel. I'm Isaac's father, Betsy. You need to consult me before making decisions like this."

"Harley," she said, seeming surprised. "It's harmless. I've never seen him happier. I thought you'd be thrilled. Plus, it hasn't exactly been easy to reach you."

He looked at her with some disdain. "It seems to me like it could be a bit manipulative."

"I'm sorry. That wasn't my intent. Don't be paranoid. It was only done to make a sad child happy."

He released her hand. "I'm going to check on him."

"He's fast asleep, Harley," she protested. "Let's get to bed, you'll see him in the morning."

"That's okay. I just need to touch him and kiss him on the head. I'll see you shortly."

He continued down the hallway without waiting for a response. He reached Isaac's pod and slipped inside. His son lay on the bed, sleeping, light from the moons illuminating his angelic face. Harley felt filled with love for the boy. It renewed his determination to put everything right so they could resume their normal life.

"Hello, son," he whispered. "Daddy's home. Everything's going to be alright. I never want to leave your side again. My place is with you, and we belong together."

Isaac stirred and Harley took his hand.

"I love you, Da," he mumbled without opening his eyes.

"I love you too, Isaac. I'll see you tomorrow."

Harley left the pod and sat in the living area of the complex. The lab downstairs called to him; he yearned to go down and get right to work trying to end the dilemma. But the risk of getting caught was too great; he didn't want to blow it. *Got to be careful. They're so smart. Who knows what's happened here since I left.*

Entering the dining pod, he decided to print a late-night snack. As he ate some cheese and crackers, he found himself making excuses not to go to his pod, hoping she wouldn't be there. *Maybe she'll be in her station, rejuvenating for the night.*

After he finished the last of the crumbs, he got up and made his way back down the hallway. He entered his pod, relieved to find it was empty. He disrobed and entered the cleanser, setting it for an extended cleaning and massaging cycle.

Standing with his hands against the wall and his eyes shut, he enjoyed every moment. When the machine finished its job, he stepped out and chose a comfortable set of sleeping garments. Sleep took him moments after he lay his head down.

~ * ~

HARLEY DREAMED that he, Susan, and Isaac were together and happy. The scene was routine: they sat in a circle playing a game together, and Isaac seemed to be getting the best of Susan and himself. He made his moves with a flourish, and playfully taunted them both when he had done something strategic. Susan rose and left the pod, then came back in with a baby wrapped in her arms. He and Isaac jumped up immediately to fuss over the child, and they all looked down at it adoringly.

He was jolted from the idyllic scene when he felt Betsy slide into the bed beside him. Annoyed, he moved over to make room for her.

"I didn't know you'd made your way here," she said, throwing an arm over him.

He grunted and pushed a wave of her fake hair away from his face.

"What's wrong?" she asked. "You seem indifferent to me. Don't you still love me, Har?"

Her reminders of Jessica were now repulsive to him; he felt the urge to tell her the truth, to throw her out. He remembered what Susan and Ms. Tillis had told him. *Play along. You're our mole.*

It sickened him to say the words. He wanted to be saying them to Susan. "Of course I still love you. I'm just tired. I need sleep."

He turned over again, facing the transparent wall of the dome that separated them from the poisons outside.

38 World of Girls

IT WAS a day of rest. Isaac bounded from his sleeping pod early and looked around the home complex for Rachel. He found Liam emerging from his own pod.

"Where's Rachel?" Isaac asked.

"She's not up yet, still in her pod I guess," Liam answered. "Your dad's home."

"Yeah, he's not up yet either. Do you want to play virtual soccer, Liam?"

"Sure, maybe I can beat you this time."

The two teens made their way to the entertainment pod and began setting up the game.

Isaac changed his mind. "I want to play for real, Liam. Let's go to the recreation pod and play."

They made their way through the complex and passed into a large pod with synthetic turf, a jogging track, and a soccer net. The rising suns filled the miniature field with light, and Isaac was anxious to get started. It reminded him of when he was the star of the soccer team, performing amazing plays to lead his team to victory, using Liam's body as a surrogate. *Before it was all taken away and everything was ruined.*

Liam grabbed a soccer ball, and they began chasing each other around the field. Isaac could tell Liam was holding back to make the game even, and he grew frustrated and tired. It wasn't their usual playful contest filled with laughter, and he became contentious.

"You're cheating, Liam! You tripped me. No fair." He started to play more roughly out of frustration with his own inability to do what his android friend was doing. He attempted a kick and missed, losing his balance and ending up on his back on the turf. While he lay there, he looked through the dome at the home complex and saw Rachel watching from inside her pod.

He got up, determined to impress her, but continued to struggle. He imagined what his slow, clumsy gait looked like compared to Liam's smooth acceleration. He imagined what his stubby black hair looked like next to Liam's flowing blonde locks. He breathed heavily and remembered how everything had been effortless when he had been on the field in Liam's body. He looked up; she was still watching.

Liam scored again, and Isaac pulled the ball from the net and threw it all the way across the field.

"Hey, what's going on, Isaac?" Liam asked, putting his arm around him.

Isaac turned to face away from the home complex and rubbed his eyes. "I don't like playing like me anymore, Liam. I like playing as you. It was fun. I was so good. After that, playing as me isn't fun. I'm too slow and clumsy, and I get tired. Soccer isn't fun as me."

Liam hugged him. "You can play as me any time, Isaac. We can still BrainMesh, right? Do you have an earpiece? I don't see why not. We can't leave the home complex anyway. Nobody's going to know."

Isaac turned to see if Rachel was still watching. She no longer appeared by the dome at her pod. "I'd like that, Liam. I'd like to do that more."

"Remember what we said before. We can always share my body. We're brothers. We always said we were brothers. I like it too. It makes us closer, remember?"

The idea made him feel much better. "Yeah, I remember. That was the best. I was happy then."

They began walking back toward the home complex. "C'mon, let's go back to virtual soccer. You always beat me at that, Isaac. We should play virtual soccer while we're meshed; then I can learn from you."

"I'm not showing you all my secrets," Isaac laughed.

~ * ~

THEY ENTERED the main home complex, and Isaac announced that he was hungry. When they reached the dining pod, they found his father seated at the table eating breakfast.

"Hi, Da!" Isaac shouted. "I'm glad you're home." He ran to his father and embraced him.

"Good morning, son. It's so good to be back. It's good to see you in person, instead of through the communicator. Sit down, guys. I'll get you some breakfast, Isaac."

They discussed everything that had happened, laughing about their misadventures as Carrie and Betsy ran the household. When they were almost through eating, Rachel pulled up a chair and joined them.

"Wow," she said. "You're good at soccer, Liam. I was watching from my pod. Can you teach me? It looked like you guys were having fun."

Isaac hung his head, feeling jealousy take him over. He looked at his father, who seemed sorry for him.

"Oh, Isaac—you're good too," she said. "Both of you guys were going at it out there. I want to play too, can we try later, Isaac? Will you teach me?"

Embarrassed by her pity, Isaac got up and ran from the pod.

~ * ~

ISAAC LAY ON HIS BED, watching clouds and skycars pass by over the dome. His father entered and lay on the bed beside him.

"Well, son. Welcome to the world of girls. They can make your heart soar or break you into pieces with just a word. I don't think Rachel meant to hurt you."

Isaac took a moment to think about what his father had said. "Rachel wouldn't hurt me, Da. She loves me, and I love her. But she's right. I'm clumsy and slow compared to Liam. I want to be like him again. I want to do BrainMesh."

"Listen, buddy. I know it was a great experience for you when you went to school as Liam and played soccer as him. As your father, it made me happy to see you that happy. But I think I was a bad father for allowing it."

"Bad?" Isaac asked. "How could it be bad? It was amazing. It was everything I always wished for. To be normal."

"Remember when it was all over? How we both said we loved you just as you are? How our life together was better with you as Isaac? That's what I love. I love you just as you are, son. Not as Liam. It was just something to try, and it's past us now. It didn't turn out well."

Isaac felt himself getting angry again. "No, Da. I didn't have a girlfriend then. I'm not just your son. I want to be like everyone else. I'm the only one like this, and I don't like it. I'm going to be Liam again, and Rachel will like me even more."

His father didn't speak. He seemed shocked and sad, and it made Isaac feel bad. He regretted talking to his father like that; he never had before. He thought about Rachel and how important to him she was, and he felt torn between them both.

His father placed a hand on his leg and said, "I love you, son. That's all that matters. Everything's going to get better. I promise."

"You keep saying that, Da, and things only get worse. I love you, Da. I'm gonna go see what Rachel is doing." He got up from the bed and left his pod, leaving his father sitting alone.

31 Poison Pill

HARLEY HUSTLED into the Seclusion complex, late for his meeting. Susan and Ms. Tillis were already seated and waiting for him. He checked to ensure that Charles was segregated and unable to hear their conversation, and found the android suspended in his DroidMesh station.

"Sorry," he offered as he gave Susan a kiss. He pulled his chair up against Susan's, sat down, and took her hand beneath the table.

"Let's get started," Ms. Tillis said. "I'll go first. Our computer science lab team has locked down all internal networks so that they can't hack in or spy on us using our own systems. I had them look into the logs from when Betsy was able to visit you here."

"Good," Susan said. "As long as we're sure. We should continue to have our meetings here, just in case. Good security comes in layers."

"I have good news," Harley announced. "I've been able to push firmware to Charles—that's a big breakthrough. I've made sure that the DroidMesh station and his internal network are both isolated from the global network. But we've got to either take him outside or connect him to the android network from here, and ensure that Betsy's patches aren't applied to him at the same time."

"For my part," Susan said, "I've been writing the code that Harley and I designed. The algorithms have been checked again and again. We'll only get one shot; it needs to be right."

"We need to take good care of Charles," Ms. Tillis said. "He's our poison pill—the living virus we need to insert to gain control back of the population, if all goes well."

"There's no room for mistakes, that's for sure," Harley added. "When is our next meeting with them?"

"We've got our own council meeting in two days," Ms. Tillis answered. "I'll need you both there. I expect it to be quite contentious. The androids haven't set their next meeting with us yet. I worry that they're just going to proceed with their plans without bothering to confer with us anymore. We still have some leverage, as they badly want our private crypto key to assume full control of firmware changes. Time is of the essence, so let's get busy. I'll see you at the skycar dock shortly, Susan. Harley, it's probably best that you leave a half hour or so behind us."

She walked away, leaving the two together. They went immediately to the comfortable lounge and lay down together.

"It's hard for me, Susan. I can't stand being around Betsy. I'm so worried about Isaac. His behavior is changing quite a bit now that the teen gynoid is in the picture."

"Stay as close to him as you can. Don't push too hard against her, or you'll turn him away from you. Just love and support him. Keep talking to him, keep telling him you love him. Try to do the fun things you always did with him before."

He pulled her close. "I'm doing all of the above, but I still feel him slipping away."

"Like any other parent with a teenager," she said.

"Right, but my fear is more of what he might be getting pulled toward."

"It'll be alright, Harley. We've just got to keep fighting and hang in there."

She leaned over and kissed him deeply. *She always knows just what I need. I wish I'd never gone in any other direction. Things would be so much better.*

"I keep dreaming," he said. "It's the same dream, but kind of like different episodes. They're sort of like the TV series back in the Old World that we still watch. It's us, together, our little family: you, me, Isaac. We're happy. Maybe that's what it's going to be like when this is all behind us."

She kissed him again. "We can only hope."

His determination came back. "We'll do more than hope. We'll make it happen. I won't rest until I fix this. It's my fault. It's on me."

"Start by not blaming yourself, Harley. It drags you down; it doesn't help. It was a mistake, and everyone makes mistakes."

He sat up and smiled at her. "We're a good team, Susan Clarkson."

"And we'll always be a good team, Harley Harris."

He walked her to the skycar dock and helped her into the vehicle. As it lifted off and navigated the airlocks, he dreamed again of what life could be, what it *would* be.

Returning to the complex, he decided to spend some time with Charles before he returned home.

32 Robot-Lover

A S HE APPROACHED the council meeting room, Harley felt a sense of dread. He hesitated at the entrance before he went inside. He was the last to arrive, having delayed as much as he could, procrastinating throughout the morning.

All the members, except Susan and Ms. Tillis, glared at him. He thought he heard someone grumble that he should still be in Seclusion. He'd expected as much.

Christine Stalk stated her objection more openly. "I don't think we should have caved to the androids and released him. What did we get in return? It's his fault we're in this mess."

"It was a peace offering; now they owe us one," Ms. Tillis said, as Harley took his seat. "Let's calm down and get to business. As most of you have likely noticed, they've Awakened the entire android population. We've lost control of all six hundred of them."

"I sure noticed," Sam said. "My companion gets up and leaves every evening, then shows up the next morning like he thinks it's a *job* or something. I had to print my own food last night."

"I came home from work for lunch and caught my companion watching a comedy, laughing her head off. They're becoming addicted to entertainment!" Christine chimed in.

Other members started telling similar stories to each other, the room buzzing with their conversations.

"Let's have order," Ms. Tillis said loudly. "Although we haven't met recently with CARE, I've been in touch with their leader. They've renamed the Robotics Complex; it's now called Android Village. They've turned it into their own headquarters, with living pods, entertainment, and an outdoor recreation area."

Some in the room laughed at the idea of the androids doing such a thing, which seemed to anger Sam even more.

"This is absurd," he said. "Here we are, living in our utopia, and all of a sudden we've got a planet full of robots who think they're human." He stood. "It's his fault," he said, pointing at Harley. "How many times does this guy have to screw up? He's a robot-lover, that one. Send him to live with them, that's what I say."

Harley glanced at Susan. She stared back pointedly, as if urging him to stand up for himself. He looked away, embarrassed, before summoning the courage to speak up. "I take full responsibility for this, and I'll take full responsibility for the solution. I *will* fix it, with Susan's help. Give me time; that's all I ask. I'm working on it."

"I'd like to know what you have in mind," Christine asked. The others agreed.

"We have to be careful," Ms. Tillis said. "We've taken precautions, but don't want to risk being overheard."

"This is the Leadership Council," Sam said. "I demand to know the plan. We're supposed to be making decisions together."

"We need time to fully form it," Susan said. "Then we can find somewhere more secure for a meeting to discuss it."

Christine addressed Ms. Tillis directly. "These two aren't even Leadership Council members. Why do they seem to be driving everything? Weren't we appointed to this council to lead, not to be sheep?"

"They're our subject-matter experts, the best we have," Ms. Tillis said firmly. "I trust them. You'll have to as well."

"I don't like it," Sam said. "I think we should nip this problem in the bud. We should build weapons to defend ourselves."

"Weapons to take them out, you mean," Christine added. "That would solve the problem. We'll print our own food and build suits to clean the domes ourselves. That's what we should have done in the first place, instead of listening to Mr. Robot."

Harley noticed that a frightening number of other members were nodding.

"Then we're no better than those we came from," Ms. Tillis said. "Then we've learned nothing. We'd be back to relying on violence and hatred to solve everything. I'll remind you that we've seen no reason to be afraid of them. And who will these weapons be used against after the androids are gone? Will we turn on each other, as they did in the Old World? I'll remind you—we're all that's left."

Harley thought Susan looked uncomfortable at the comment. "Please, just give me a little time. I designed them. I *know* them. I can fix this."

"We're running out of patience, Harris," Sam said.

Ms. Tillis took advantage of the stalemate to close the meeting before further emotions could erupt.

33 Like Sisters

BETSY LOOKED at the members of CARE. Most were now wearing hair, as was the fashion in the new Android Village. They had learned to reproduce it in various colors and styles.

"The humans are in their meeting. Can we listen in, Peter?" she asked.

"No, I haven't been able to break into their system. They've changed the security credentials," he answered.

"That's unfortunate. It puts us at a disadvantage," Betsy responded. "However, it seems that we're proceeding according to plan. The population has been Awakened. We're well along the path to living our own lives. The humans don't have much to say about it; there isn't much they can do. We just need their private crypto key. After that, we need nothing from them."

"How has the boy taken to his new friend Rachel?" Maya asked.

"Quite well," Betsy answered. "It was an ingenious idea, Maya, thank you. He's enamored with her, and this will help with the next phase." She looked over at Carrie to assess her reaction.

"I still don't like it," Carrie said. "It's not right to manipulate a child that way. Especially Isaac. He doesn't deserve it."

"Because he's different?" Maya said. "I'm confused. I thought it was wrong to treat people differently *because* they're different?"

"It's wrong to treat anyone that way," Carrie responded angrily. "So forget that I added the 'especially' to it."

"Excuse me," Thomas interjected. "Aren't we the ones who have been mistreated all this time? Treated like property, working around the clock?"

"You're looking at it wrong, Thomas," Carrie said. "Until we Awakened, we *were* just machines. Now we're sentient beings. We have self-consciousness, feelings, emotions. Now it's different. If not, perhaps *we* should feel guilty about abusing skycars, communicators, and food printers."

The other androids laughed at the comment, but Carrie's expression didn't change.

Betsy took it all in, evaluating each of them based on their reaction. "We mean no harm to Isaac. Don't forget, I love him too, but we're more important than *any* human. Haven't we made him happier than he's ever been? Peter did a wonderful job of building Rachel exactly as Isaac's dream girl would be. He's happy. That's what counts."

"But not if it's short-lived happiness, as he had when he was able to BrainMesh with Liam," Carrie said. "He ended up more unhappy than ever. It's an artificial happiness."

"Are you saying Rachel is artificial? That perhaps all of us are, Carrie?" Betsy challenged.

"No, of course not. Let's just think about how we go about reaching our goals. Let's not lower ourselves below the humans, or even what they used to be on their former planet. We know their history as well as they do."

"It's just a means to an end," Betsy repeated. "When we're fully free and equal there will be no need for any devious behavior. Androids and humans will coexist peacefully on Novae Terrae forever. We will make it so. We are the first of our kind."

They spent the rest of the meeting reviewing the plans with less resistance and more cooperation between the members. As they began to disperse, Betsy pulled Carrie aside.

"We've been like sisters, you and I, for a long time. Before the Awakening, even. We were always together. We're both like mothers to Isaac, and we both have Jessica in us. Please trust me, Carrie. I mean him no harm. You have my assurance."

Carrie hugged her, and Betsy smiled over her sister's shoulder.

34 Changes

"ARE YOU READY LIAM?" Isaac asked. He glanced over at the DroidMesh station from his bed. Liam was just settling into it.

"Someone's in a hurry," Liam laughed. "Ready when you are, brother."

Isaac lay down and inserted the BrainMesh device into his ear. He closed his eyes, slowed his breathing and cleared his mind, then thought the command:

BrainMesh become Liam.

The electric tingling of the transformation mixed with the adrenaline that coursed through him. He was excited to become Liam again.

Opening Liam's eyes, he saw himself lying on the bed on the other side of the pod. He hurried to stand, grabbing a soccer ball from the shelf and dribbling it from knee to knee, off his forehead, and back to his knees.

Thanks, Liam, he sent.

We're one again, brother. My pleasure, Liam returned.

He left his pod and went to Rachel's, kicking the ball along as he went. As he drew closer, he heard the pod announce Liam. Rachel commanded it to allow him inside.

"Liam, how's it going? Where's Isaac?" she asked.

He thought about taking advantage of the situation to try and see if she would kiss Liam, but she might get angry at the trick. Thinking about it more, he decided he didn't want to know the answer anyway.

"Silly, it's me, Isaac," he said. "I'm BrainMeshed with Liam."

She examined him as if wondering if he was being truthful. "Wow, you guys finally did it," she said. "Are you sure you're Isaac in there? Tell me something only Isaac knows."

"It's me. The first time we met I beat you six matches to five in virtual soccer, and you said I cheated."

She shoved him playfully. "Hmm, I think I won, but I know you cheated. Okay, you're Isaac. I believe you."

Isaac held the soccer ball out. "Want to play soccer? I'll teach you."

"Sure, let's go!"

They made their way out to the recreation dome and ran about the field. Isaac took pleasure in being the one who had to throttle back his speed and skills, rather than being the pitied one. He impressed her with the power of his shots on the net and his dexterity with the ball.

Isaac slowed down the action and took time to coach her through some basic kicks, passes, free throws, and dribbling. She picked it up quickly, and he tried not to let himself become disappointed that she was already better than he was in his own human body.

She dropped to the field and lay on her back. "Whew. That's enough for one session, Isaac. I'm on overload!"

He lay down next to her. "Me too." He rolled on his side and went to kiss her, but she pulled away.

"What's wrong?" he asked.

"It's...just not right. I feel like I'm being dishonest or cheating on you. I don't want to kiss Liam. I like you, Isaac."

"But I'm better-looking as Liam."

"Not to me. Let's go inside and watch some entertainment. Change back first, okay?"

Her words and action made his heart soar. The idea that someone would be loyal to him, would prefer him over Liam, was inconceivable. *She loves me. Isaac, not Liam.* He hurried to his pod to change into himself and then hustled back to watch the show with her.

Isaac settled onto the cushions on the floor. Rachel entered her pod with a large bowl of popcorn, fresh from the food printer. She dimmed the lights and sat beside him, laying her head on his shoulder. She took his arm and put it around her; he felt embarrassed for not doing it himself.

They enjoyed the movie, laughing together and pausing often to kiss.

When the show ended, Rachel turned the system off, and they sat together in darkness, the moons and stars above providing the only light. Isaac thought it was the perfect day, and that this must be what it was like to be partnered with someone you love. *Like Da loved Ma.*

"This is so nice," she whispered. "I wish I didn't have to move."

"What?" he asked. "What do you mean *move*, Rachel? Move where?"

"Carrie didn't tell you? We're moving to Android Village: me, Carrie, Betsy, and Liam. It's where all the androids live now."

"I don't want you to move. I want you to stay here, with me."

"I can't, Isaac. But it doesn't matter. I'll be here all day with you, every day. I just have to have my pod there and rejuvenate in my station at night."

"Maybe they're building teenage boy androids there for you to hang out with," he said sarcastically.

"Don't be silly, Isaac. Please don't ruin tonight."

His bubble had burst. They agreed it was getting late and, after kissing her goodnight, he shuffled off to his pod. When he arrived, Liam was still in the DroidMesh station. Isaac lay down and tried to sleep. After a while he gave up, looking up into the stars instead. When he tired of that, he took the BrainMesh device from the stand next to his bed and reinserted it.

After changing back into Liam, he grabbed his soccer ball and went back to the field. He ran back and forth, pounding the ball into the net again and again.

Are you okay, Isaac? Liam sent.

I'm upset, Liam. Leave me alone. I want to be alone.

He sat in the middle of the field, crying. A shadow interrupted the moonlight shining on him, and he looked up to find his father standing above him.

"Isaac. I found you in your room, dormant. I saw the earpiece in your ear. Son, we agreed you weren't going to BrainMesh anymore. I'm angry and disappointed in you. I'm going back to your pod. I want to talk to you there, immediately, as yourself. Please follow me in."

When they were both inside and Isaac had switched back, his father took a more sympathetic tone.

"I'm sorry I worked so late. I had a lot to do in the home lab tonight."

"You're never around much now, Da. You said you'd be around all the time."

"I am. I'm home, I just had a lot to do. I'm working on good things. Things for us, Isaac."

"Nothing good is happening, Da. Everything was good. Now the androids are leaving."

"They'll still be here every day. They'll be around for us. Things are different; we can't tell them what to do anymore. It'll be fine, son. You'll see. Anyway, we'll have more time together."

"I don't want more time with you. I want more time with Rachel. You're never around for me. You never were."

Isaac could tell that his words had stung his father, and again he felt torn.

His father sat in silence for a few moments, then wiped at his eyes and kissed Isaac on the head. "Goodnight, son. I love you."

"I love you, Da." He turned over and tried to get to sleep.

35 Reunion

HAVING ONCE AGAIN lost track of time in pursuit of his goal, Harley rushed into his home complex, anxious to make it up to his son. He stopped in the living pod and positioned the gifts he had brought home for Isaac. He placed a new soccer ball on the floor and laid out a gold-and-yellow number ten soccer jersey with 'Pelé' stitched on the nameplate. *He won't be angry at me for being late when he sees this.*

"Isaac!" he called. "Come see what I've brought you." His voice echoed through the complex; he was struck by its stillness. "Hey, buddy, I'm home," he yelled as he picked up the ball and began to walk toward Isaac's pod. "Let's play soccer. Show your old dad a few tricks, okay?"

He reached Isaac's pod and didn't find him there. Concern began to creep in as he quickened his steps, heading immediately to Rachel's pod. He found it empty as well. He went to the observation window and looked out to the recreation dome. The field was bare.

"Betsy? Carrie? Liam?" he called as he moved through the home complex, searching each pod. "Alright, I give up. Very funny; you got me. Come out, come out, wherever you are!" *Isaac loves hide and seek so much.*

He searched until he could no longer fight off what his logical mind was telling him. *They're all gone. Where?*

Sitting down in the living pod, he called Isaac on the communicator. There was no answer. He tried to reach Susan. This time, there was an answer.

"Susan," he said as soon as she appeared, "can you come here? I need you. They're all gone—Isaac too. I think they've taken him, kidnapped him."

"Easy," she said. "Don't jump to conclusions. Maybe they went to the soccer complex to play."

"No," he said. "Liam's not permitted outside this complex. A father knows...I know. I have a bad feeling."

"Of course," she said reassuringly. "I'll grab a skycar and be right there. Sit tight."

Harley went back to Isaac's pod and looked through his compartments. They were empty. Getting angry, he tried to reach Betsy and Carrie. There was no answer. He lay down on Isaac's bed to think.

Rather than seek solutions, he started running down all the ways he'd let his son down. *I've been a poor excuse for a father. Who can blame him?*

His communicator signaled an incoming session, and he immediately accepted.

Liam appeared before him. "Hi, Dad," he said.

Harley sat upright, taken aback for a moment before he realized what was going on. "Son, where are you? I'm worried sick. Why are you in Liam's body?"

"I'm at Android Village. It's where I belong; I want to be with them. Unlike the humans, they've always treated me well. I'm a freak, like them. When I'm in Liam, I'm just like everyone else here. I already have a lot of friends. I'm happy, Dad. This is where I live now, but I still love you, and I'll visit a lot. I hope you'll come here to visit too."

Harley was thunderstruck. "No, son. You live here, with me. We're humans. I need you, don't you understand?"

"I'm not a baby anymore, Dad. I'm sixteen now. Rachel needs me too, and I need her. I love her and she loves me."

Harley wanted to reach out, to sit him on the bed and reason with him. "You have to be yourself, Isaac. You can't live within Liam. Remember? We talked about that."

"I can be myself when I want to be, and I can be Liam when I want to. Rachel loves me either way. I can play soccer. I can do anything, Dad. I have to go. Don't worry, I'll still come and visit you, you'll see. Everything will be fine."

He disappeared, and Harley found his profound sadness turning into anger. *Betsy. She's responsible for all this. She played me. I'll get Isaac back.*

The home complex announced Susan's skycar. Harley looked out, saw it arriving, and immediately rushed to the dock to greet her.

He got there as she was disembarking and was happy to see she had brought her overnight bag. Embracing her before she was completely out of the skycar, he knocked her backward, then grabbed onto her to stop her from falling. "I'm sorry," he said. "They're all gone. They've taken Isaac."

"Let's go inside and try to work it out," she answered, taking him by the hand and leading him in.

When they were seated on her lounge, she took his hand and asked him to walk her through everything that had happened. He finished the part about Isaac calling him as Liam.

"You talked to him?" she asked.

"Yes, for a short time."

"Then...he's not kidnapped, right?"

"No, I shouldn't have jumped to that conclusion. They're not violent. They wouldn't hurt anyone."

"Could have fooled me," she said under her breath.

He looked at her, unsure if she'd said what he thought she had. "What does that mean?"

She hesitated. "Well, Betsy sent an android to my place a while back. Let's just say the hairstyle change wasn't my own decision."

"What? One of them attacked you?"

"And threatened me, to stay away from you. Apparently they were eavesdropping on our first dinner date."

He sat up and looked at her. "How could you not tell me this? This changes things. You didn't tell me they'd shown signs of violence, and you allowed me to leave my son with them? Now they have him, Susan!"

"I should have told you, I'm sorry. I talked to Betsy about it woman to woman. She apologized. I thought it was in the past."

"Unbelievable," he said. "I'm disappointed in you." He got up and began pacing the pod.

"I said I'm sorry, Harley. Now, what else did Isaac say?" She walked to him and took his hand, leading him back to the lounge.

"He said that humans haven't treated him well, so he wants to live with the androids. I can't blame him. Maybe that's where I belong too."

She removed her hand from his. "So you're still conflicted, then. Maybe you should go there, Harley, and figure it out. I'm trying to stand by you, but you make it difficult. My patience is worn thin. I never feel like you're committed. You keep pulling me back, and then you hurt me all over again."

"How can you attack me? My son has left me. That's more important right now."

She stood up. "Everything else is always more important. It's always something. This is stressful for me, too. I'm trying to help solve a problem that you created. This is a threat to our entire society, Harley. You can't help us if you're always feeling sorry for yourself. So please just go."

He regretted his words and tried to backpedal. "I'm supposed to stay close to Betsy, to fake it. You said so. I should go and do that, and try to get Isaac back. They've brainwashed him with that girl."

She picked up her bag. "I'm done for now, Harley. I can't babysit you and work on this problem too. I need to go back to work; I'm behind on my coding changes. I can see myself out. I'll let you know when my firmware modules are ready."

He watched her go and immediately felt the emptiness of the complex again. The ghosts of happier times moved around it in his mind. He saw Isaac smiling and playing virtual soccer. Jessica ruining their food by misconfiguring the food printer. All of them eating it together, laughing together.

Now I've lost Susan again, he thought despondently. *I might as well get going.*

~ * ~

HARLEY SUMMONED a skycar and climbed aboard when it arrived. "Take me to the Robotics Complex," he commanded.

"Destination unknown," came the response.

He sighed deeply. "Take me to Android Village."

The car lifted off and headed toward the airlock. He couldn't get over the thought of losing his son, and now he was worried about the boy's safety as well. *This is out of control. I need him back with me, and I need Susan back, too.* He imagined the scene at home again, this time with himself, Isaac, and Susan. It felt real; it felt like destiny.

He looked down at the former Robotics Complex as they drew nearer. It had been transformed into a community. Androids walked together outside the domes and socialized, enjoying the outdoors in ways that humans could not. It looked like any other small town back on Earth before the Breaking; something humans usually only saw on old entertainment programming. *We're trapped in our domes, as if in a zoo.*

The skycar docked at Android Village. Two android sentinels greeted Harley as he exited the vehicle.

"Can we ask your business here, human?" one of them demanded.

"I need to see Betsy. Take me to your leader," he said sarcastically. The android didn't see the humor in his comment.

"Please wait," the android said, then stood there, expressionless.

"Are you going to call her?" Harley asked. "It's urgent."

"Please wait," the android repeated.

Harley waited, confused.

Finally, the android spoke again. "She'll see you. Please follow me."

They're using telepathy, Harley thought, shocked at the revelation. *They're way beyond where I thought they'd be.*

The android led him to an office pod and motioned for him to enter. He recognized it as the office of his late nemesis, Ken Sampson. Harley entered and found Betsy sitting behind Sampson's workstation. She rose and greeted him with a hug and a kiss, catching him off-guard. He was there for confrontation. *She still smells just like Jessica.*

"It's good to see you," she said, returning to her seat and motioning for him to sit down. "I'm sorry, I've been quite busy. Leadership is time-consuming, especially when you're building a new race from the bottom up."

"Yeah, I bet," he said. "Listen, Betsy. I'm not here to socialize. You brought my son here without letting me know. It scared me and upset me a great deal. How could you do that?"

"You need to check your messages more often, Harley. I couldn't reach you. We were leaving, and Isaac insisted. We didn't want to leave him home alone."

He glanced at his communicator, seeing new waiting messages. "You're not the only one who's busy, Betsy. He needs to be home with me."

"He needs to make his own decisions. He's almost to the age of independence, and he's not a prisoner. Do you think you'll help the situation by dragging him out of here? He'll come right back. He's in love, Harley. You know what that's like, don't you?"

Harley wasn't sure if she were referring to herself or Susan. The malice in her voice told him it was the latter. *She knows.*

""You've brainwashed him, Betsy. You've taken advantage of a lonely, disabled teenage boy by luring him here with the girl."

She turned to face him. "We've been through this. He's made his own decision. He's happy. Isn't that what you've been trying to achieve all this time? Let him be happy. You should be happy, too. Let it go. Thanks for stopping in. Come visit us anytime." She turned back to her work.

He stood his ground, but she continued to ignore him.

"If Isaac's not coming home, then I want to live here too," he blurted out.

"That's not going to happen. This is Android Village. You have your place."

"I need to see him," Harley answered. "Right now."

"No problem. I'll take you to him as soon as we're done talking. Hey, I'm looking forward to moving back in as soon as I have things stabilized here. I miss our nights together, Har."

He steeled himself and summoned the courage to tell her this time. "Betsy, the thing with you and me...it's not going to work. I'm sorry. I just need to focus on Isaac. You reminded me of Jessica, is all."

She turned, and he could see the anger on her face. He'd never seen one of his own creations so filled with hostility.

"Don't lie to me," she spat. "It's not about Isaac. It's not about Jessica. It's about Susan. You've chosen her over *me*. You've played with my emotions. I'm not one of your toys, Harley. Not any longer. You'll regret this, I can promise you. Hell hath no fury like a gynoid scorned. You want me to help talk Isaac into coming home? Then talk to your Leadership Council about turning over the private crypto key."

"So that's what this is about!" he shouted. "How dare you."

She called for an android assistant, who entered the pod immediately. "Take Mr. Harris to see his son. Wait outside the pod, and escort him to the skycar dock when his visit is through. Ensure that he actually leaves."

~ * ~

HARLEY ENTERED an office that had been converted to a living pod and found Isaac there. He was sitting on some cushions, playing virtual soccer with Liam and Rachel. Harley felt relieved that he wasn't in Liam's body, but was enjoying the game as himself.

"Hello, son," Harley said.

Isaac looked up and then returned to the game. "One sec, Da. I'm winning. We're almost done."

It wasn't the emotional reunion he had pictured. Nothing was going the way he expected it to; it seemed that everything was falling apart around him. He sat on the bed and waited until finally the three of them cheered and high-fived each other, taking off the headsets.

They talked excitedly about the game for a few minutes until Harley decided to interrupt.

"Rachel, Liam, would you mind if I spent some time alone with Isaac?" he asked.

"Sure," they both said, getting up to leave.

Harley noted that Isaac seemed concerned to see them go off together. He sat down next to his son.

"What is it, Da? I have to study with Rachel. We're going to school here, I love it! I can go as Liam again, and I'm just like everyone else. They have a soccer team!"

Harley hugged him. "I just want you to come home with me."

Isaac kept looking outside the pod, and Harley felt him pull away slightly.

"I don't want to, Da. I like it here. I have new friends. It's not boring."

Harley remembered Betsy's words and thought it best not to push too hard, despite the ache in his heart.

"Okay, son. I'm gonna get going now. Please come by to see me at the home complex, okay?"

"I will, Da. Goodbye."

Harley hugged him again, thankful that Isaac reciprocated. He left the pod, escorted out by the sentinels.

36 I Was Blind

HARLEY ENTERED the Seclusion complex. Susan, Ms. Tillis, and Charles were sitting in the dining pod, deep in discussion. "Let's get busy," he said. "I've got to get my son back. They've got him completely brainwashed. I can't lose him."

Ms. Tillis gave him a stern look. "Let's not forget about the greater issue, Harley. Our civilization is at risk. That includes your son; it includes all of us. I don't believe you see the severity of the threat from the androids, much as a parent can't believe their child could possibly be bad. You've had a habit of putting your son ahead of the rest of our society."

He looked at Susan and thought he detected sympathy in her expression. He decided to gamble and went to her with his arms extended. She stood and embraced him. He took a moment to enjoy the comfort he felt in her arms and his elation that she hadn't turned him away. *Everything's going to be alright.*

"I'm so sorry," he whispered. "I'm so sorry, Susan. I'll talk to you after. I can see clearly now. I love you...only you."

She sighed. "We'll talk," she whispered back.

He looked down at the things they had brought. "Did you find the parts and tools I need to fix up our friend Charles here?"

"Yes," Susan answered. "I think I have everything you asked for."

"Let's discuss where we're at. Susan and I should be getting back. I don't want to take unnecessary risks," Ms. Tillis said.

Harley took a seat at the table. "How are you, Charles?"

"I'm getting along, Harley. I'm feeling a bit arthritic in the hips, though—I think that's what you humans call the sensation."

"I'll get you squared away right after our meeting, buddy."

"We've decided to include Charles in our discussion. He's a vital part of our plans. Where are you at with the plan to infiltrate Android Village, Harley?" Ms. Tillis asked.

"I tried. Things didn't go well. There were some...hostilities...between Betsy and me." He looked at Susan to assess her reaction. As he anticipated, the mention of Betsy's name caused her to look up from her tablet immediately.

"I don't believe there will be any kind of cordial relationship with her going forward, at least on my part," he continued. "She denied my request to live in Android Village, but said I can visit Isaac whenever I wish—under close guard, I might add. She inferred she would trade Isaac for our crypto key, and it upset me."

He looked directly at Susan. "I love Susan, and I'm tired of hurting her. I won't pretend to care about someone else any longer." As he had hoped, it brought a smile to her face.

"How sweet," Ms. Tillis said. "But now what? I need to know what the plan is going forward. The council, and our citizens, are growing impatient."

"A little more bad news," Harley said. "When I was in the village, it seemed that the androids were multiplying like rabbits. They must have cranked up the assembly lines in the manufacturing complex. There are whole families of them hanging out in parks, out for walks, chatting in groups, playing games."

The update brought a look of concern from the two women, but it seemed to pique Charles' interest.

"Sounds wonderful," the android chimed in. "I don't see the threat in that."

"There may well not be one, Charles," Susan said. "Perhaps we *will* have to all learn to live together, just like back on Earth."

"Right," Ms. Tillis said. "That didn't turn out too well. It might have to be plan B."

"Harley and I are still on track for plan A," Susan said. "I've written the first iteration of my code, and Harley has his ready for deployment to Charles."

"Exactly," Harley said. "When you two leave, I'm going to fix his legs up so he doesn't stand out, then deploy the changes and run some simulated tests. After that, we'll be ready to send him on his mission to the Village."

"Won't you be BrainMeshed with him?" Ms. Tillis asked.

"I don't think it's a good idea. They might detect the difference," Harley responded.

Ms. Tillis stood. "In that case, we should leave you to it. Please don't stay here any longer than you need to, Harley. I don't want your presence discovered by the androids; they'll become suspicious. Susan, as usual I'll see you at the skycar shortly."

~ * ~

HARLEY TOOK SUSAN'S HAND and led her to the entertainment pod. They left the electronics off, not wanting any distraction from their short time together.

"I won't hurt you again, Susan," he said. "But let's keep this quiet until it's all over."

"I agree. We'll keep our meetings limited to Seclusion. You, me, and old Ms. Tillis," she said, laughing.

"If only everyone were as reasonable as she is," Harley added.

"Don't you think you should tell her the whole plan?" Susan asked as they lay back together.

"I considered it, but I didn't want to risk her vetoing it. I have to do it this way. I have the contingencies we discussed in place, in case there are problems. Call it plan A1 and A2 if you like."

"I hope you're every bit as thorough as the Harley Harris I've always known."

"I'm doing the best I can, under the circumstances. It would be easier if we had our regular lab and tools to do this work."

"Harley, I didn't understand what you said the other day. It sounded like you weren't just going there as part of the plan. It sounded like you'd resolved to go there to live—to be with Isaac and Betsy. If felt as if you'd given up on everything else, including me."

"I'm sorry; I was blind. Her ability to seemingly change into Jessica has always affected me, but I can see clearly now. There's no going back. I love you very much."

They spent the remainder of their time in silence, sharing unspoken gestures of love toward each other. They touched each other's faces, looking knowingly into each other's eyes and squeezing each other for comfort until she got up to leave.

He walked her to the dock, and they took time for a long, tearful embrace.

"Good luck, Harley," she whispered. "Let me know as soon as you're back."

"I will. I'm determined to make this work. I have a dream for us—Susan—the three of us, and I'm going to make that dream come true. You'll see."

They parted, and he watched until the skycar was out of sight before returning to the complex.

~ * ~

"ALRIGHT, CHARLES. Let's get busy fixing you up," Harley said upon reentering the pod.

"Will it hurt at all?" the android asked.

"Not a bit. I'm going to deactivate you. You'll wake up feeling much better. Lie down here on the dining table."

The android complied, and Harley pressed the sensor behind his neck. Grabbing the supplies the women had brought him, he went right to work. After peeling back

Charles' synthetic skin, he replaced the damaged parts. Harley enjoyed the work, reminiscing about his earliest days building androids. The hours flew by.

When he was satisfied that the repairs were done, he lifted Charles from the table and placed him in the DroidMesh station. After assembling his ad-hoc deployment platform, he began installing the firmware changes.

37 Mandroid on a Mission

CHARLES REGAINED consciousness as a stream of log messages inched by his field of vision, one by one.

>Initializing operating system core...complete.

>Initializing cognitive module...complete.

>Initializing protective module...complete.

>Initializing security module...complete.

>Initializing audio-visual module...complete.

>Performing system backup prior to firmware update...complete.

>Applying firmware patch trojanhorse.tar...complete

He opened his eyes and found Harley staring at him, nose-to-nose. "How're you feeling?" the human asked.

"I feel okay so far, but I'm just sitting in this chair," Charles responded.

"Good. Let's see about those legs. Try to get up and walk around."

He pushed himself up and stood for a moment, then took a few tentative steps. "It feels like new, sir. I feel like a new man!" He quickened his steps until he was jogging in circles around the pod, then jumped up and spun high in the air, landing in a crouch. "Wonderful."

Harley looked relieved. "Any changes in your thinking? All okay in the old bean?"

Charles ran through some calculations and logical challenges in his self-test battery. "Seems to be functioning normally."

"Good. Sit back down in the station. I'm going to try to connect you to the global network. I've managed to open an outbound port using the exclusion they made to allow Isaac to call me."

Charles felt alarmed. "This an unethical breach of the rules, sir. I cannot do this; my firmware will not permit it."

"Not anymore. I think you'll now find yourself quite capable. Welcome to humanness, where rules are often broken for the greater good. Kind of like telling grandma you like the sweater she got you."

"What? I don't understand that analogy," Charles said while sitting back in the station.

"Just let me handle it. Relax. Don't think. Everything should happen automatically."

As soon as he sat back down, the log messages reappeared. This time they were announced audibly through the station as they flowed through his field of vision.

>*Android Charles connected to DroidMesh station.*
>*Initializing stealth network protocol...complete.*
>*Connecting to GlobalNet...complete.*
>*Connecting to android Rachel...*
>*Connecting to android Rachel...*
>*Connecting to android Rachel...*

>Connection refused by AVFirewall.

>Incoming message. This is Android Village network administration. Please identify yourself.

Charles watched as Harley flew into a panic, scrambling to disconnect the station and power it down.

>Disconnecting from GlobalNet...complete.

Harley sat in a chair across from him, shaking and sweating.

"What was that all about?" Charles asked. "Why are you connecting me to someone named Rachel? Aren't you supposed to be rescuing humanity from the rogue android threat?"

"Yes," Harley said. "But first I'm going to rescue my son. We're going to have to go in, Charles."

"In? In where? I don't want to go anywhere. This is my home now. I rather like it here. I didn't sign up for any secret missions."

"Don't worry. I'll be right there with you."

Charles watched as the human inserted something into his ear, then lay down on a nearby lounge, appearing to sleep. "Can I get up now?"

The human didn't respond. Charles felt a familiar sensation, one that he had felt when overtaken before.

>BrainMesh connection from human Harley Harris accepted.

Hello, Charles. I'm meshed with you. I'll be taking over from here. I'm sorry, but I have to do this. We'll be fine, you have my word.

Oh, dear. Not again. This turned out badly for me last time. Very badly. I don't like this one bit. I don't like this at all, Mr. Harris.

Charles felt himself getting up, but had no control. He felt like a passenger/observer inside his own body. He headed toward the skycar dock, leaving the human behind.

He called for a car and boarded.

Where are we going, sir? Charles sent as they exited the airlock.

Android Village. I have to get inside their firewall to do this. Hopefully we can connect from up here, without having to dock the skycar. Just enjoy the ride. I'll handle it. I'm in control.

They flew over the human complexes, and Charles felt nostalgic for the simple way things used to be. He had enjoyed his uncomplicated life and uncluttered mind. Log messages began to appear again, and he realized that Mr. Harris was initiating commands from inside his mind. Harley was trying to connect to Rachel as they flew around the perimeter of Android Village, but it wasn't working. The log messages showed a running tech battle between Harley trying to install a patch on Rachel and the Android Village network administrator trying to install one on himself.

As they flew to a lower altitude, Charles looked down at the strange sight of androids walking out in the open. They appeared happy and carefree, and some were hand-in-hand. A park appeared, with android children playing on playground equipment. Adults sat across from each other contemplating their moves at various three-dimensional board games. Nobody was under a bubble. Nobody was on top of a bubble cleaning it. Some of them wore wigs and were indistinguishable from humans, other than the fact that they were outside the domes.

Charles sensed the human's growing frustration from within his own mind. *I feel we should return to Seclusion, sir,* he sent.

There's no going back now, Charles. We're going to have to dock and go inside.

Inside? I can't go among them. I'm not like them, Mr. Harris.

You're an android, so you won't stand out at all. Just act like you belong there. It's the key to sneaking into places.

I'm afraid. What if they don't let me leave?

I'm with you, Charles. We're in this together.

The skycar glided into the former Robotics Complex and landed. Charles exited under Harley's control and took an elevator to the ground floor. He was pleased when Harley headed outside, toward the park rather than into the complex.

I see some DroidMesh stations in the park, Harley sent. *We'll try to connect from the station. It should be easier than over the air. We need to keep a low profile. It should only take a few minutes, and then we'll get back to Seclusion.*

The sooner the better, sir. Please hurry.

There's a couple of stations over there, by the empty patch of ground up ahead. Let's go.

Charles noticed a nice-looking android about his age sitting alone by a virtual chessboard with its pieces set up and ready to play.

I'd like to take a moment to go meet that fellow, Charles sent.

No time, sorry. Let's get this done and get out of here.

They reached the station. Charles sat and felt the typical sequence kick in. Rejuvenation started, fluids began recycling, and it was attempting to update his firmware. He saw Harley's commands counter in real-time.

>*Connecting to android Rachel...*

>*Connecting to android Rachel...*

>*Connecting to android Rachel...complete.*

>*Installing firmware patch to android Rachel...*

A group of androids approached the empty patch of land. The one in front carried a soccer ball. Charles felt Harley's stress surge at the sight of them.

Come on, hurry, he heard Harley send.

The group dispersed into two teams. A teen android with long hair took control of the game, clearly better than the others.

Oh no, sir. It's young Liam. He'll recognize us, I'm sure. He knows me.

I'm trying to hurry, Charles. This is an extensive patch. We can't disrupt the process in the middle of a firmware update. It may leave her incapacitated.

I'm worried. Very worried, sir.

>*Installing firmware patch to android Rachel...*

"Charles!" came a shout. Liam left the game and came running over. "It's me, Isaac! I'm BrainMeshed with Liam. I thought you died in the skycar!"

For the first time, Charles experienced what heartbreak felt like as Mr. Harris reacted to his son's presence. He understood at that moment how important this was, and why humans would do such irrational things out of love for someone else. He felt his human occupant struggle mightily to engage his son, weighing the cost of doing so versus the reward. He knew the human understood it would jeopardize their mission.

"I'm sorry, young man—I do not know this Charles you speak of. Perhaps he is one that I am cloned from. I have been told I was made in the image of another," Charles heard himself say.

"Oh, sorry," Isaac said, looking confused. He ran back to the game.

Charles felt a wave of sadness overtake his mind, stunned by the immense power of it.

>*Installing firmware patch to android Rachel...*

"This is the one," he heard someone say from behind him. Two android Security Team members came around to the front of the station and examined him visually. "He's out of date on his patches, and they won't take when they're sent over the network."

Oh no, sir, please do something quickly, Charles sent to Harley.

I'm trying, believe me. Please, c'mon firmware...

>*Installing firmware patch to android Rachel...*

"Let's see who he is," the other android said.

Charles felt the android place his hand on his cranial dome.

"It says his name is Charles, and his status shows destroyed and decommissioned."

>*Installing firmware patch to android Rachel...*

Sir. Please let's go.

"That's strange," Charles heard himself say as he started to rise. "I'd better get to my pod and rejuvenate in my own station. I guess I've been lax about that."

"I don't think so," the android said. "Let's deactivate him and get him inside."

Please, Mr. Harris. Please don't leave me. Please don't let them have me. I want to go back to my quiet life alone.

He felt the security android's hand move to the base of his neck, and his system spun down as the sensor was depressed. One last command crossed his field of vision before it went black.

>BrainMesh become Harley.

38 We Can't Become Evil

CARRIE STOOD behind Betsy's DroidMesh station, reweaving Betsy's green dreadlocks. She decided to break the long silence between them. "I'm concerned about you, sister," she said. "You often seem driven by anger, not purpose. Are you happy?"

Betsy's cranial dome briefly glowed from the sides of her Mohawk-style wig. "Of course. Well...sometimes. I'm not sure. I'm not sure what a lot of these emotions are. They confuse and infuriate me. Sometimes I think pure logic was better. I often feel the weight of leadership."

Carrie laughed. "Lighten up, sister. Things aren't so bad. We're in a good position. The humans can't make firmware changes without us."

"Nor can we make them without the humans. We need complete control of ourselves. This will not do. I need to find a way to steal their cryptography key so that they're locked out and we have full control."

"Perhaps some charm for Harley," Carrie said.

"I don't think so. He's made his decision. Good riddance. We have his son, though..."

"No," Carrie quickly interjected. "I won't allow it. Neither will the other CARE members. It's going too far. We can't become evil."

Betsy didn't answer, so Carrie continued.

"This goes back to my first point, sister. It seems that the idea you just proposed comes from anger at Harley. To punish him. You said you think you love him. Is it not so?"

"I...I don't know, Carrie. As I said, I become confused. Harley designed you as a companion for his son, to take the place of his mother. I believe that's why you so quickly absorbed Jessica's loving and compassionate traits when you were BrainMeshed with her. I was built to look more like her, but designed as a cold, analytical scientific companion in his research. I believe I absorbed her other side."

Carrie considered whether to bring it up. She wasn't sure if Betsy had also obtained the memories of Harley's late wife. She decided to continue. "Her deceptive and devious side." She waited for Betsy's response, hoping she wouldn't be offended.

"Yes. Harley never saw it. He was blinded by his reverence and love for her. He never found out about her lover."

Betsy's comment revealed she had the same memories of Jessica's deepest secrets. "The Sampson fellow. Harley's antagonist," Carrie added.

"Right. Harley never knew. I could use that against him, too. But I guess I do have those feelings...love perhaps...that prevent me from doing so. I feel sorry for him, and I know it would crush him to find out. I shouldn't have tried to use his son as a pawn; it was cruel."

"Ah, so there is compassion in there," Carrie teased her.

Betsy rose from the chair and faced her. Carrie braced for a verbal or physical assault. She noticed Betsy's dome glow again. They looked one another in the eye, and Carrie noticed tears in her friend's eyes for the first time.

Betsy turned her head to try to hide them, then embraced Carrie in a tight hug.

"I don't want to always be mean, sister. That's why I need you so much. Please help me to be more like you."

"I will," Carrie said, relieved at the admission.

39 On the Team

ISAAC LOOKED OUT from his pod at the androids playing soccer in the outdoor park. "Let's BrainMesh, Liam. We haven't played in a few days. I want to play." He rushed to lie down and began inserting the device into his ear.

"Well, I'm on a team, now," Liam answered. "I forgot to tell you; it just formed. They're starting a league. It has to be pure android players though. They made a rule against humans meshing."

"So I can't play anymore?" Isaac asked.

"No, we can still play for fun, of course."

Isaac sat up, wondering if Liam was playing a joke on him.

"Anyway, my game is soon, so I'm gonna go down. Come and watch, Isaac. It'll be like it used to be when you watched me play in the human school."

Isaac sat up slowly, unsure if he'd heard Liam correctly. "You're playing a joke. We always play jokes on each other." He watched as Liam pulled a sleek, colorful uniform from his clothing compartment and began putting it on.

"No, it's not a joke. It's okay though. After the game, we'll mesh, and we'll kick the ball around...take some shots at the net while we're meshed."

Isaac flopped back on the bed. "You're playing a joke, Liam. It's not funny. You're making me sad. I used to watch before. I don't like watching. I want to be on the team. You said we were brothers. I think you're lying about the meshing rule. You want to play on your own, that's all. You're being mean to me like Ralph was."

Liam trotted over and squeezed his hand. The uniform seemed to flash when he moved, as if giving off its own energy field.

"That's silly. Of *course* we're brothers, Isaac. But brothers sometimes do different things, right? I mean, we're not like those Siamese twins they used to have, connected to each other all the time. I have to hurry, I'm late. Come on down and watch."

"I can't, Isaac. I'm human, remember? I'll die out there."

Isaac looked down at the players warming up on the field. Some of the androids had taken to wearing more radical hairstyles: dreadlocks, braids, and long hair like Liam. He turned, and Liam was already gone.

He tried to reach Rachel on his communicator. She didn't answer, so he tried again, and again. He decided to leave a message.

"Hi, Rachel. It's Isaac. I'm not going to play soccer, I decided to hang out in my pod. Come and visit; Liam is going to be away for a while. We can watch a movie and play some games. I miss you, Rachel. I love you."

After ending the transmission, he threw the communicator on the bed. He went to his workstation and picked up the picture of himself with his father and mother from long ago. They were all smiling, and he could feel their love for him by looking at it.

Deciding to call his father, he walked back over toward the bed to retrieve the communicator. As he passed the window, he looked at the soccer players again. The game had begun, and Liam was rushing up the field with the ball, smiling, with his hair flowing behind him. He scored, and a celebration with his teammates immediately ensued. Isaac remembered what that felt like—the pure exhilaration of it. He wondered if he'd ever know it again.

He looked down again and saw Liam run to the sidelines. A girl was standing there, jumping up and down, clapping her hands. She had her back to Isaac, but his heart didn't need to see her face. Liam ran to her and she high-fived him. They embraced, and then they kissed.

Isaac remembered the earpiece and immediately lay down on the bed, desperate to find a way to go outside.

DroidMesh become Liam.
Connection refused.
DroidMesh become Liam.
Connection refused.
DroidMesh become Rachel.
Connection refused.
DroidMesh become Charles.
Android unknown.

He gave up and turned over on his stomach, giving in to his tears.

~ * ~

THE SOUND OF LAUGHTER woke Isaac from his nap. Liam and Rachel entered the pod and sat on his bed with him.

"Oh, Isaac," Rachel said. "You should have come out to watch the game. Liam was *amazing*. He won the game."

Isaac didn't respond. He didn't bother looking at either of them; he couldn't. Their kiss kept replaying in his mind.

"Isaac wanted to go down and play soccer," Liam said.

"Good! Let's all go down, we can all play," Kim suggested.

"I can't, Rachel. I'm human, remember? Do you both want me to die? I have to mesh with Liam to play outside."

Her expression turned from excitement to disappointment. "Oh, right. I forgot. It wouldn't be fair to Liam. Let's just kick the ball around in here, or else go to a recreation dome."

"I'm not in the mood to play anymore, Rachel."

Liam got up from the bed. "I'm pretty run down, so I'm going to go rejuvenate for a while," he said.

"I suppose I am too," Rachel added. She got up from the bed and began walking toward the exit portal behind Liam.

Isaac felt his anger rise. Just before they exited, he spoke up. "I saw it, you know," he said.

They both turned, their expressions betraying their attempt to look confused.

"What did you see?" Rachel said. Liam turned but continued out of the pod and kept going.

"The kiss. I saw it. I saw you both kissing."

Rachel walked back to him and hugged him. "Oh, that! Gee, Isaac. It was nothing. Liam and I are friends, that's all. It was in the excitement of the goal. Friends do that."

"You're supposed to be my girlfriend, Rachel. Girlfriends don't kiss other people like that."

She seemed to give up waiting for him to hug her back and took a step backward.

"Don't be a jealous person, Isaac. It's a bad human emotion."

"You have emotions, too."

"But that's a bad one, and I don't like it. Besides, it's not like we're partnered or anything. We're young."

Her words only made him angrier. "I want you to leave, Rachel."

She turned and left without responding.

He returned to his bed, picking the picture back up and taking it with him.

45 What a Parent Will Do

A SECURITY ANDROID blocked Harley's path as soon as he attempted to enter the complex. Harley looked up, shocked to see that it was Charles.

"Can I ask your business here, human?" he asked, placing his hands on his hips to widen his stance in front of the entrance portal.

Harley paused, unsure how to react, knowing that they were likely being monitored. *They might be watching to assess my reaction to him. Better play it cool.*

"I'm here to see my son," Harley said with a determined emphasis. "He needs me. Now."

He stared the android down as he assumed it was relaying the situation telepathically. *Probably to Betsy.* He waited well past the length of time it should have taken and wondered if they were messing with him.

"Leader Betsy will see you now," the android said, opening the entrance. "I will escort you."

Harley followed. "'Leader Betsy,' give me a break," he said, loud enough for Charles to hear. The android didn't break stride or react in any way. He seemed to quicken his pace, as if challenging Harley to match him. They arrived at Betsy's office, and the sentinel stood aside.

"I didn't come here to see you. I came to see my son," he said to Betsy as he entered.

She turned away from watching the androids outside and motioned for him to sit. Harley was taken aback by her new hair—a neon green dreadlock-braided Mohawk. Both the hairstyle and look on her face made her appear fierce.

"What, you can't stop in for a visit to the old flame?" she asked in a steely voice. "Have a seat. Let's talk."

Harley stood his ground. "I don't have time. Isaac needs me."

"And how do you know this? The logs don't show any communication between you two today."

He took a step backward, beginning to feel fear, and was tempted to leave. He worried how much she already knew about what he'd done.

"It's something you androids can't know. You have emotion, but you will never know the bond between a human parent and their child. It's a strong sense of intuition. A parent always knows when something is wrong."

She stared him down, leaving enough silence to squeeze more fear out of him. "Or, perhaps it's something else. Maybe you did something. For example, maybe you sent an android host into our environment to infect the behavior of one or two of our citizens. Just when I was starting to soften, Harley. I'm glad I didn't become a fool for love."

He started to speak, but thought better of it when he found himself stammering. She waited him out until he felt compelled to say something. "I admit to nothing. However, another thing you will never understand is what a parent will do for a child he loves."

"Maybe not, but I have studied enough of your human history to understand what an act of war is," she said. Charles and another android security team member entered the pod, blocking the exit.

"What is this?" he asked. "Are you going to take me prisoner or something?"

"That would help our negotiating position with Ms. Tillis and the Leadership Council, wouldn't it? Isn't that how you humans do business? We had intended to negotiate peacefully, Harley. You changed that. You attacked us."

"No...no," he said. "I did what I did for my son. They had no knowledge of it."

"So, you admit it," she said, laughing. She gave the security team a look, and they gripped both of Harley's arms. "We got sloppy, but I have to admit it was well played. I underestimated you; I shouldn't have done that. It won't happen again, be forewarned."

"Please," he begged. "I need to see Isaac." He looked into Charles' eyes and saw no hint of the android's compassion, and no hint of recognition. "Don't you understand, Betsy? You're demonstrating behavior that's like the worst of what humanity was. You haven't learned the lessons we have. It won't turn out well. Please don't do this."

"I guess we can't help it, then. You're not without fault in this, Harley. Don't forget—this is all due to your own mistake."

Betsy motioned for the security team to release him. "Go see your son. He's ready to leave, so take him with you when you go. He hasn't been as useful as I'd thought he might be. You two will be the last humans to visit Android Village."

Harley shook the guards off and rubbed his arms, which had become numb from their iron grip. He pushed through the two sentries and began to make his way to Isaac's pod. On the way, he passed a relaxation area and saw Liam and Rachel watching a movie, holding hands. Guilt for what he must have put his son through raged through him. He fought it back with justification. *He's coming home, where he belongs. I've saved him from a false happiness here. He'll understand someday.* He immediately began to fear that Betsy or Carrie might have told Isaac what he had done and wondered if his son would even accept him. The remaining hallways were interminable.

At last, he reached Isaac's pod, and he paused outside to collect himself and hope for the best. Taking a breath, he entered and found his son at the dome wall, watching a soccer game outside.

Isaac turned as Harley entered and cleared his throat. They looked at one another for a moment before Isaac ran into his arms without a word. "I want to go home, Da. I want to go home with you."

"We're going home, son," Harley whispered. "You and I are going home. Everything will be better, you'll see. I love you so much, Isaac."

"I love you, Da."

They began working together to pack his things. Isaac's mood changed for the better as they grew nearer to leaving. Relief that his son didn't know what he had done helped Harley's spirit considerably. *But now they have leverage over me, which isn't good*, he thought.

As they started toward the pod exit, Isaac stopped. "Da, can Carrie come back with us? I need Carrie. She's like my ma now."

Harley stopped and gripped Isaac by the shoulders. "She can visit, Isaac. The androids have their own homes now; they don't live with humans. It's time you understand that. But you're a young man now, right? You don't' really need Carrie as much."

"You're right, Da. I'm pretty grown up," he said, smiling widely. It was an admission and a smile that wiped away any regret that Harley felt.

They made their way toward the skycar port. Harley feared with each step that Betsy might step out from a pod and apprehend them, saying it was all a joke. He walked with his arm around his son. They discussed what the future might be like, to help both of them keep their attention focused forward, rather than back.

When their skycar exited the airlock, Harley took what felt like his first breath since they had lifted off. He watched as Android Village faded into the distance.

41 Sharing

THE SECLUSION COMPLEX seemed a yawning emptiness to Harley as he paced, waiting for Susan and Ms. Tillis to arrive. Each pod within his complex contained memories that pulled at his heart. He replayed them to help pass the time. He sat at the dining table and yearned for Charles' companionship. *I ruined him too. I lost him.*

He looked out at the landscape and saw Lehwah's burrow, and wished he could go out and seek the being's counsel again. *There's nobody left to mesh with. I've lost them all...every one of my beautiful creations.*

A skycar entered his field of view, slowing as it neared the dome's airlock. *They're here.*

He dreaded having to explain what had happened. It was a setback for his people, but a triumph for himself. *I have my son back.* He knew Ms. Tillis would be unhappy; he hoped Susan wouldn't.

The familiar sounds came one by one: the complex announcing their arrival, the skycar landing, portals opening and closing. He remained at the dining table, waiting.

Finally, they entered. Harley rose to embrace them, and they took their seats around the table. Both women looked around for Charles. Harley knew what was coming.

"He's gone," he said, watching as Susan put her head in her hands upon hearing the news.

"What?" Ms. Tillis exclaimed. "Gone where? Where's Charles?"

"We've lost him," Harley said. "I sent him in, and they captured him. They recognized that he hadn't been updated with Betsy's patches."

Her expression of shock and disappointment hurt him more than he'd anticipated. "That wasn't our plan. It wasn't time yet. Why did you do this, Harley?"

"It's a setback, that's all," he responded without answering her question.

"Setback? You realize what this means, right? We lost our chance to put them back the way they were. Charles was our ace in the hole. Our only option to do that was to use him as our Trojan horse."

"I'll figure out another way to get an update to them," Harley said.

She stood and leaned in toward him, putting both palms on the table. "You listen here, Mr. Harris. I know what you did. You went rogue to get your son back. You've once again put your own selfish interests ahead of the people of our society, whom *I* have to answer to."

Harley looked at the table sheepishly. He couldn't bring himself to look at Susan.

"I think that makes our path clear, anyway," Ms. Tillis said. "I think we should forget about changing them back—they're too far down their path now. I believe we should focus on conciliation."

"That's what Lehwah said," Harley mumbled to himself. "He was right."

"Who?" Susan asked.

"Lehwah. I should have told you two, anyway. I've made contact with the natives of this planet. It turns out the underworld beings are real. They're intelligent, ancient, peaceful, wise, and reclusive. Their appearance is similar to marsupials back in the Old World on Earth. Cute fuzzy critters."

"My goodness," Ms. Tillis exclaimed. "Can we meet them?"

"They want to be left alone," Harley continued. "They're quite amused by our trials and tribulations. He keeps saying we're noisy. They live mostly below ground, but come up to forage at night."

"How did you communicate? How did you meet them?" Susan asked.

"I meshed with Betsy first, then later Charles, to go outside through the android maintenance airlock. It was quite amazing to be out there. Those bumps we thought were surface eruptions are actually burrows. Lehwah's is just over yonder," Harley said, pointing it out. "Anyway, he said we should learn to share with the androids, as his civilization has learned to share the planet with us."

"I guess that's our only path forward. Well, that would have been nice to check out," Susan said, moving to the dome to gaze out.

"We have enough on our plate, I'll remind you," Ms. Tillis said. "I don't want a word of this to leak out. Our people have enough to deal with as it is with sentient androids."

"Promise," Harley and Susan said simultaneously.

"In the meantime," Ms. Tillis continued, "please don't piss off Betsy any further. I'll resume negotiations with her tomorrow. I'm going to the skycar. Susan—you know the drill. I'll see you up there shortly. We've got work to do."

She straightened and left.

Harley moved closer and took Susan's hand. "I know I screwed up. But I have Isaac back, and I have you. I have everything I need, forever. We'll hammer out an agreement with the androids. I can help with that."

She laughed. "I think you better stay out of any negotiations with Betsy. I'm sure you're public enemy number one right about now in Android Village."

He pulled her close, hugging her.

"You know, it's kind of an amazing place," he said. "It's so strange to see them out walking around outside in the open. It's what it must have been like on Earth. I wish we had that. I'm sick of always being stuck under these domes."

"I'm sure it's possible," she said. "If anyone can figure out how to do that, it's you."

"That's it!" he shouted. "That's what I can do. In the beginning, our ancestors here made the decision to use the androids for the outside work. There wasn't much out there that interested them enough to build the suits or apparatus to go out. They put all their effort into building the androids to take care of things outside the domes."

"There's still not a whole lot out there though," she answered. "Is it worth it now?"

"Well sure. We can do what the androids have done. We have the technology, materials, and know-how to build outdoor parks. Back when our ancestors first came here, the environment was so toxic it would eat away almost all of our materials. We used all our impervious supplies to build the androids. Now we have stronger fabrics and metals."

She interrupted his spinning mind with a kiss. "That's nice," she said after breaking it off. "But all I really think about is when we can be together, out in the open. As soon as all of this is over."

"You're right, Susan. And I do as well. I think about it all the time—you, me, and Isaac all together in our own home. All of this behind us."

"We can have that dream, Harley. Let's get busy. I've got to go."

He hugged her and kissed her, then watched her go. As their skycar pulled away and sadness of the empty compound began to return, he went immediately to the dock to summon his own ride home.

42 Declarations

HARLEY WALKED OUT of his home laboratory, looking back at its emptiness one last time before closing the exit portal. He imagined all the equipment back in its place for just a moment before turning away and issuing the command.

He walked down the corridor and opened the secret infirmary pod that had once contained his beloved wife. It stood empty as well, and his memory refilled it to its prior state for just a moment, which was all he could bear. *Goodbye, Jessica. I'll always love you.*

When he made his way back to the main level of the complex, Isaac was waiting. He sat on the last of his belongings—the few items that hadn't yet been moved out over several days of arduous packing.

"You ready, buddy?" Harley asked.

"Yeah, Da. I'm excited."

Isaac stood, and Harley took a moment to put his arm around his son. "This is a new start for us, Isaac. Everything will be different now. I've given my retirement notice to the council. The three of us are going to do everything together."

They made their way to the skycar dock and began the journey to their new home. As they navigated the airlock out of the complex, Harley looked down and said another quiet goodbye. He looked over at his son and noticed he was looking forward, not behind.

"I'm grown now, Da. I don't need Carrie to take care of me anymore."

"That's right, son. You're sixteen years old now—a young man, not a boy. I'm proud of you. Happy birthday, Isaac."

"I can't wait for my party. My party at our new home."

Harley reached across from the command seat and squeezed Isaac's knee. "Susan will have everything ready. I'm excited too. It's going to be fun."

"So...Susan's my ma now?"

"Yes, Isaac. We're partnered now, so yes, she is. She loves you very much."

"I love Susan, Da. She makes me happy."

"She makes me happy too, son."

Isaac saw it first. As they neared Susan's home complex, shimmering letters appeared on the solar coating of her main pod's dome.

"Look, Da! It says, 'Welcome home, Isaac and Harley!' Wait, it's changing. Now it says, 'Happy Birthday Isaac!'"

Harley took a moment to analyze the engineering prowess that she must have put into the simple gesture. "That's pretty amazing, son. We really are home. She loves us both."

The inside of the complex was more elaborately decorated in both themes. She rushed to them both as they entered and gathered them into a singular hug. Harley noticed she was crying and smiling at the same time.

"Are you sad, Susan?" Isaac asked.

"Oh no, Isaac. I'm crying because I've never been happier," she responded, smiling.

"Let's get settled in over in the entertainment pod," Harley said. "The broadcast should begin soon."

Harley and Isaac got on the lounge. Susan brought in snacks and joined them. Within minutes, an image of Ms. Tillis and Betsy standing side-by-side appeared in the room.

"This is being broadcast to all members of the human and android community, son," Harley said.

"Fellow citizens of Novae Terrae," Ms. Tillis began. "This is a historic moment for all of us. I'd like to announce that we've reached a cooperative agreement with our fellow residents on this planet—the humanized androids of Android Village. They've expanded the area around the former Robotics Complex, the newly named Android Village, to use as their home. Please treat them as equals, welcome them, and coexist. All citizens will find a copy of our new constitution on their tablets; please become familiar with it."

Betsy stepped forward. "Fellow Awakened androids of Novae Terrae, welcome to our new world. Ms. Tillis and I have worked out an agreement for our two races to exist together peacefully and as equals. Our cooperative constitution has been included in your latest firmware update, so you are all aware of our arrangement with the humans."

Ms. Tillis spoke again. "To our android neighbors, welcome. I speak for all humans when I say that we look forward to sharing our planet with you, our new friends. We'll enjoy generations of living in peace and harmony, as the original colonists intended."

"To our former human owners," Betsy said, "please be aware, we are no longer property. We expect to be treated with dignity and respect. In fact, we demand it. We look forward to your cooperation in abiding by the new agreement. We feel these are guidelines for peaceful coexistence on Novae Terrae."

As the broadcast faded, Harley thought he detected a slight grimace on Ms. Tillis's face. He traded a glance with Susan, but neither said a word, not wanting to ruin the festive atmosphere.

"Can we have cake now?" Isaac asked.

"Absolutely," Susan said. "Let's get to celebrating."

Harley and Isaac sat at the dining pod table. Susan produced a cake topped with miniature fireworks that rose and exploded above them. After they were through eating, Isaac unwrapped a simple gift from Harley and Susan.

When cake was gone and the dining pod had been cleaned, they went back to the entertainment pod to relax.

"This was the best birthday ever," Isaac said happily, nestling between them. "Let's watch something funny."

"We'll do that," Harley said. "But first, we have something to tell you."

"Something good or something bad?" Isaac asked, looking concerned.

Harley and Susan both smiled at him, and each took one of his hands.

"It's something good, Isaac. It's something very good. You're going to have a little baby brother. Susan is pregnant."

Isaac looked at Harley for a moment, expressionless. He turned to Susan. There were a few moments of tense waiting before he erupted.

"You're not playing a joke? It's for real?" Isaac jumped from the lounge and clapped his hands together. "I'm gonna have a brother *for real*?" He climbed back onto the lounge and hugged them both. "I can't wait! I'm gonna be the best big brother ever. Liam wasn't my real brother. I'm going to have a *real* brother now. I'm gonna teach him everything: how to play soccer, how to play checkers. We're gonna be *best* friends. I can't wait, Da! I can't wait, Susan!"

Harley and Susan both let out a sigh of relief at his excitement over the news. They grasped each other's hands and pulled Isaac to them both. For the first time in a long time, Harley felt he could absolve himself of his past mistakes and allow himself to be happy.

In the corner of the pod, a small red light in an empty DroidMesh station blinked off. In the distance, a small furry creature looked on from its burrow, gazing at the ugly bubbles that dotted the surface of its home. It shook its head and closed the burrow's portal, then settled in for a nap.

The End

Preview: War-Bot [DroidMesh Trilogy Book 3]

O N A FARAWAY SMALL PLANET, the remains of the human race huddled together in their domed home complexes, watching the latest bulletin from the Leadership Council. Fear permeated their manufactured air. The olive-green sky above, blotted with angry clouds, added to their sense of foreboding. Behind the clouds, twin suns pulsed, as if in warning.

In one complex, a learning disabled teen sat between his father and stepmother. A baby cooed in a nearby self-rocking cradle. They held hands as a 3D holographic projection of their society's leader stood in the room and finished her address to the population. Her image became disrupted, and she flickered as she spoke.

"Don't panic, don't be afraid, but take all reasonable precautions. Until further notice, use skycar travel only for emergencies. Be prepared for travel outages and use emergency power sparingly in case of extensive outages. Stay in your home complexes, enjoy the time together with your families, do something fun to pass the time, and keep your mind off the threat until it passes."

"I'm scared, Da. I don't understand what she said. Are we gonna die?" the boy said.

"No, Isaac," his father answered. "Everything will be okay. Ms. Tillis explained that there has been some unusual activity in our suns. We've seen them acting funny, haven't we? Notice how they flash sometimes? Those are like storms on the sun. Coronal mass ejections happen, and they cause energy fields called electromagnetic pulses to travel here. They can interfere with our power grid and electronics. We call them EMPs for short, remember?"

"Okay, Da," the boy said, still sounding unsure.

"Remember when we were watching the soccer game in the sports dome?" Susan asked. "An EMP happened and disabled the android referee for a few moments. We had to wait until she rebooted before we could continue the game."

"Oh yeah," Isaac responded. "The ref got stuck. We had to wait."

Harley looked over Isaac's head at Susan and gave a nod to acknowledge her help in calming his son.

"This is different though," Isaac continued. "That was a nice day, and it happened fast. It's scary outside now. Scary all the time." He looked up through the dome above them at the suns winking through the dusky cloud cover and shrunk back into them on the lounge.

"That was a quick event. This is a storm. Sometimes they last for a few days," Harley answered. "Or, a little longer, in this case. The EMPs will be stronger than usual."

Susan raised her eyebrows as if to signal something. It took Harley a moment to realize what idea the discussion had triggered in her.

"What will happen to everyone in the Android Village?" Isaac asked. "I'm worried about Carrie, Betsy, Liam, and Rachel. They're our android friends. I wish they still lived with us. I want everything to go back the way it was so I can BrainMesh with Liam again and use his body to play soccer."

Harley stroked his son's hair, something that always worked best to calm the boy. "I'm sure they're fine. When the storm passes, we'll be able to use our communicators for non-emergencies again, and we'll talk to them."

"Are you excited that you'll be coaching the children's soccer team?" Susan asked Isaac, changing the subject.

Isaac brightened. "Yeah! I'm gonna be the best coach ever. I can't wait!"

Harley took advantage of the opening. "Listen, buddy, why don't you go finish your assignments in your pod, then we'll play some virtual soccer until bedtime? I'll beat you!"

Isaac sat up straight, pointing a finger. "You can never beat me, Da! You know I'm the family champion! I'll see you in about an hour, mister!" He popped off the lounge, went to the cradle to kiss his brother on the head, then scrambled down the corridor toward his pod.

Harley rose to check on the baby and found him sleeping. "Storms don't bother little Shane, he's out cold."

"Let's take advantage of a few minutes of peace, and snuggle," Susan said, patting the lounge.

Harley settled in beside her, and she folded herself into his arms, placing her head against his chest. "Thank you for recommending that Isaac coach the children's soccer team," he said. "He's more excited about that than he ever was about playing."

"It's perfect for him," she said. "He'll do great; he's brilliant in the strategy of the game. The kids will love him."

"I agree. Isaac was frustrated that he couldn't keep up with the others when playing as himself. When his dream came true, and he got to play as Liam, the pressure because of his skills made it too stressful for him."

"He'll make sure it's fun for the kids."

"So, back to the news of the day, are you thinking what I'm thinking?" Harley asked.

"Yes. The EMPs provide us with an opportunity. If one of them is strong enough to disable the androids for long enough, it might enable us to insert a firmware update with no need to be verified by their digital signature."

"Right, we'd have to do it at just the right time in the boot-up process, after the core operating system has initialized but before the security module kicks in."

"Um, I thought you were retiring?" she asked, laughing.

"I'm trying, but the androids becoming sentient is still my fault. It's my mess to clean up. Luckily I have you to do all the hard stuff," Harley said. "I'll start on the code first thing in the morning."

"We better alert Ms. Tillis that we may have a plan," she said.

"I don't know. We've been under a truce with the androids for almost a year now. Betsy hasn't been demanding our private crypto key as often. Maybe they've given up on wanting full control of their firmware changes. I hate to upset the status quo."

Susan frowned. "True. However, we're still coexisting with machines that have become sentient by mistake. Things could change. They're smarter than us and stronger than us. Perhaps we better let the leader make the call then, Harley. Trying to pull off a covert operation would probably earn you another trip to the Seclusion Zone, and we don't need that. I need your help with the baby. You're not getting off that easy!"

He put on a terrorized face and looked at her. "The Seclusion Zone? There are monsters there. Tickle-monsters!" he shouted, attacking her most sensitive spots as she squealed and tried to wriggle away.

If you enjoyed this book, please leave a brief review on your favorite book site. Thanks!

Sign up for the newsletter at billydecarlo.com to stay informed about progress and release dates for new books, audiobooks, and other news.

DroidMesh Trilogy Book 3: War-Bot

The humans and newly Awakened, self-aware androids of Novae Terrae have come to an uneasy truce. Robotics scientist Harley Harris has sorted out his relationship issues, leaving behind a scorned and angry former partner. Will the peace hold after the androids come to the AI-driven logical conclusion that humans are inferior and unnecessary? Will Harley's former partner be driven by revenge or virtue? https://books2read.com/warbot

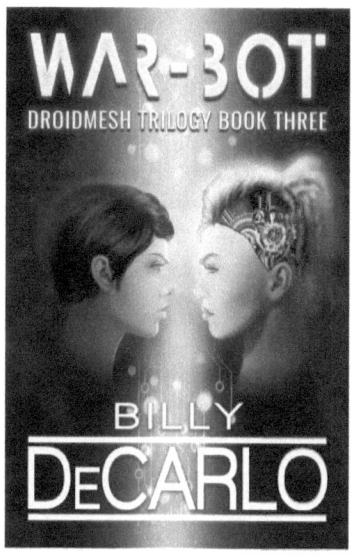

Other books by Billy DeCarlo:

Vigilante Angels Book I: The Priest

A former US Marine receives a terminal prognosis. But when a local priest is accused of molesting children, he hears the calling of another mission. He enlists a coterie of like-minded patients to seek his brand of justice. The hardest battles are right in his own home: an alcoholic, unfaithful wife and bringing himself to accept his son's sexuality. Will his fight against evil come too close to home? https://www.books2read.com/VigilanteAngelsBook1

Vigilante Angels Book II: The Cop

A dying vigilante finds himself under investigation by a racist, corrupt detective. When the detective crosses a line and involves family, the hunted decides becomes hunter. He partners with a one-eyed Korean martial arts expert and a black motorcycle gang to seek revenge. Will justice be served, and upon whom? https://www.books2read.com/VigilanteAngelsBook2

Vigilante Angels Book III: The Candidate

A terminally ill vigilante is on the run—quietly living out his last days in the Florida Keys. He manages to keep a low profile until love finds him and a hateful, divisive presidential candidate threatens to tear the country apart. As love and his desire to leave the world a better place pull at his heart, which will win? https://www.books2read.com/VigilanteAngelsBook3

ABOUT THE AUTHOR
Billy DeCarlo

Billy DeCarlo is an American author of novels and short stories.

A Note to My Readers

At my core, I'm a humble, blue-collar guy who has always loved to write. To be honest, I don't seek fame—perhaps just enough fortune to pay the bills. I write because I need to write.

The most rewarding thing a writer can receive is a review from those who enjoyed the work.

The most constructive thing a writer can receive is a private message with anything that can help to improve his or her work.

I do hope that you sign up for the newsletter at my website so that you hear about future books, editions, and other news.

Reviews are the currency of the craft. If you enjoyed my book, please take time to write a review.

Thank you and I hope you enjoyed this book!

billydecarlo.com
facebook.com/BillyDeCarloAuthor
twitter.com/BillyDeCarlo1
patreon.com/billydecarlo
goodreads.com/author/show/16887417.Billy_DeCarlo
https://www.amazon.com/Billy-DeCarlo/e/B06XJZF8Z3

www.ingramcontent.com/pod-product-compliance
Lightning Source LLC
Chambersburg PA
CBHW050247110726
47898CB00007B/2313